NEWES
from the
DEAD

BEING A TRUE STORY OF ANNE GREEN

HANGED FOR INFANTICIDE AT
OXFORD ASSIZES IN 1650
RESTORED TO THE WORLD AND
DIED AGAIN 1665

MARY HOOPER

DEFINITIONS

NEWES FROM THE DEAD
A DEFINITIONS BOOK 978 1 862 30363 8

First published in Great Britain by The Bodley Head
an imprint of Random House Children's Books
A Random House Group Company

The Bodley Head edition published 2008
Definitions edition published 2009

1 3 5 7 9 10 8 6 4 2

The Random House Group Limited supports the Forest Stewardship
Council (FSC), the leading international forest certification organization.
All our titles that are printed on Greenpeace-approved
FSC-certified paper carry the FSC logo. Our paper procurement policy
can be found at www.rbooks.co.uk/environment.

Set in Hoefler

Definitions are published by Random House Children's Books,
61–63 Uxbridge Road, London W5 5SA

www.kidsatrandomhouse.co.uk
www.rbooks.co.uk

Addresses for companies within The Random House Group Limited
can be found at: www.randomhouse.co.uk/offices.htm

THE RANDOM HOUSE GROUP Limited Reg. No. 954009

A CIP catalogue record for this book is available from the British Library.

Printed and bound in Great Britain by CPI Bookmarque, Croydon, CR0 4TD

Thanks are due to the present owners of the
Great House at Dun's Tew, to Oxfordshire
Studies at the Westgate Library, Oxford, and
to the Oxfordshire Record Office. Most of all
they are due to my agent, Rosemary Canter,
and Sarah Ballard, in-house editor, both of
United Agents, who were unstinting in their
enthusiasm, ideas and encouragement.

PART ONE

CHAPTER ONE

It is very dark when I wake. This isn't frightening in itself, because most of the year I rise in darkness, Sir Thomas insisting that as much as possible of the house be put in order before any of the family are about. It is the quality of the darkness that is strange; blacker than black, soft and close about me.

I go to turn my head towards the window, to see if any streaks of light can be seen in the sky, but my head doesn't move! I try again, and again. I lift my hand – or try to – but that doesn't want to obey me either.

I conclude that I must be deeply asleep, in some sort of trance-like state, and aware that I'm dreaming. I think I will just wait for it to pass so I may rise, dress and go about my household duties.

The waiting continues, and I feel nothing: neither cold nor warm, hungry nor replete. I just sense the blackness and soaring emptiness, but this is not too unpleasant. Some time later, but I cannot tell how long, I perceive movement across the backs of my eyes: four blurry white streaks, moving and gliding in the blackness. The streaks are feathery soft and remind me of doves, or the soft, enveloping wings of angels. The blurry shapes move across my eyelids but when I try to stop them, to endeavour to focus on one and see if I can spy a shining halo or a gold harp, I find it impossible.

I would like it to be angels that I dream of, for I know that would be very lucky. The Reverend Coxeter told us that. He said that no matter whether you are a scullery wench or a lord in his castle, you are truly blessed if you dream of angels. I have tried to dream of them ever since I heard that, but have never succeeded.

Suddenly I remember something and want to scream with terror, and the blackness loses its velvety softness and takes on an aspect of such vast and unknown fears that the angels disappear. What I have remembered is this: the last time I saw the Reverend Coxeter 'twas not in church, but in a bleak yard in the icy rain, and he was entreating the Lord to have mercy on me, preserve my soul and convey me quickly to Paradise. Behind him had been a great crowd of people, a mighty wooden scaffold from which hung a heavy, knotted rope and a man wearing a black hood. And it was for me that all these were waiting, for I was . . . was about to be hanged.

A terrifying thought comes to me: If this happened, *am I now dead*?

No, I cannot be, for surely I can hear my heart thumping within me and echoing through my ears.

Then is this the state which they tell us about in the Bible. Is this purgatory?

What happens when you're there?

I struggle to think and recall that purgatory is said to be a painful state, with tortuous fires to cleanse the soul and bring it to righteousness. But how long does it last, this purgatory? A very long time, I think – thousands of years.

My state is not painful *now*, though, so perhaps it might not be too terrible to be in purgatory. If it just meant lying here quietly in the dark, it might be quite bearable. There would be no rising at two in the morning on washing day to soak the linen, no more scrubbing of the kitchen range until my hands bled, no more going without food for breaking a plate and being unable to sleep for hunger. No more of *that*, either – that which Geoffrey Reade sought. As I think on this, I feel a shadow pass over my soul and know, without being sure of the circumstances, that he is inexplicably connected to my fate now.

I leave this thought a-tremble in the air and move on. Yes, I could, perhaps, bear purgatory. What I cannot bear

. . . what I won't contemplate is . . . no, no! I won't let that thought in. But it comes anyway: *What I could not bear, dare not consider, is the possibility that I'm not dead, but merely occupying a coffin, having been buried alive.*

I'm of a sudden desperate to come out of the trance I must be in, for surely – oh, surely – I am still in the little bedroom I share with Susan, and merely deeply asleep. I urge myself on. In my mind's eye I picture myself pushing back my coarse blanket, swinging my legs out of the bed and rising up, but though the urge is there, though I think I can perceive my muscles trembling with the effort to work, nothing happens and no part of me moves.

I concentrate harder. Maybe sitting up is asking too much of my body. It will be enough if I can move my hand, feel what's around me: the straw mattress beneath me and the blanket on top. Once I know that I'm safe in my bed, I'll be content to lie here longer.

I realize then that instead of being in my usual sleeping position, curled up like a woodlouse, I'm lying straight and still with my hands crossed over my breasts. But this is not the usual manner in which I go to sleep . . .

My limbs are not working but my mind is going ahead, whirling on a dance, showing me images of the effigy in St Mary's: a stone woman lying with her arms crossed over her cold stone body. Indeed! That's how they lay out the dead!

I'm so disturbed by this image that I forget to breathe for a moment.

I open my eyes; close them again. It makes no difference to the quality of the darkness. In fact I don't know if I'm opening my eyes, or just dreaming I'm opening them. Am I asleep or awake? Alive or dead? Am I already a cadaver?

My heart contracts with terror at this thought; there is a pain behind my eyes where I long to cry and a choking in my throat, but it seems that even crying is denied me. I begin to count to calm myself down. It is what I learned to do when Master Geoffrey was— But no, I cannot think on that yet.

I wonder if this state, this condition of mine, is punishment for what I have done, for they are very hard with all who commit sin now and I have heard of women who have fornicated being tied on a ducking stool and dropped into a pond, and those who have stolen being whipped round the village behind a cart. I have never heard of anyone being buried alive, though.

I am very, very frightened. If I find out that I am buried I'll claw at the wood which surrounds me, scratch the walls of my coffin and break out. But what will I do *then*? If I'm a buried corpse, then I'm under six feet of earth and will never get free. Best to die quickly perhaps, to clamp my lips together, stop myself from drawing breath and perish.

In the blackness behind my eyes I try to see the blurry shapes again and turn them into comforting angels, but I cannot. Instead, chunks of my life come crowding in, clamouring to be listened to, asking that they be considered in order to make sense of what's happened to me.

So to start. It seems to me that going to work for Sir Thomas Reade was the beginning of it all, for that was how I came to be acquainted with his grandson and his heir, Master Geoffrey Reade. His name evokes a terror, but I don't want to think why. Not yet. It is ahead of me though, a source of shadows in my head, waiting to be explored.

But surely not all my recollections of that household are painful? There must be some which are not, I think, and I scuttle through my mind, throwing up memories like fallen leaves, looking for the bright ones.

I have been working for the Reades since I was but a young child and, this titled family being the most noble in the area, 'tis thought a great honour to serve in their household. They own several estates in the county of Oxfordshire, and at first I worked for them at Barton Manor, a vast dwelling in Steeple Barton, the village where I was born. This village contains about a hundred people who mostly work on the land and is a small but ancient place with farms and cottages, bakers and blacksmiths. At one time it also contained a gracefully ordered church, but that was before Cromwell's men tore down its altar rails and broke its windows and pretty statues to turn it into a bare meeting house.

Being well-taught by my ma as to cleaning, washing and the making of soaps and scented waters, I began working at Barton Manor as a scullery maid. This meant that I was the lowest person in the household and had to heed the wishes of everyone, which – if two persons had opposing wishes – was sometimes very difficult. I soon got to know the ways of the Reades, however, learned how to walk softly about the house so as not to disturb them, to bob a neat curtsey and to discourse with lowered head if addressed by a member of the family. I can remember some good days then, for life seemed easier in the old house and we servants had an amount of freedom. In Maytime there was always a pole on the village green to be danced around with ribbands. In the summer we'd while away hours cherry-picking in the orchard and gathering soft fruit – raspberries, strawberries and mulberries – eating as much as we collected in our baskets. Later in the year, when the harvest was in, there would be a dance in the servants' hall with a fiddler paid for by Mr Peakes, the butler, with his own money, and we'd have a merry time dancing most of the night. We always sang as we worked at fruit picking or scrubbing or scouring: old songs we'd learned from home and ballads that the pedlars sold, and so my first two years with the Reades, before the war started, passed quite pleasantly, for I was but a child then and my wants were few.

The big house, however, Barton Manor, was burned to the ground during an early battle in the Civil War, and two of Sir Thomas's sons died during this skirmish, for they fought for King Charles – which was to say they fought for the losing side. When I think of our King Charles, he who was beheaded, I suddenly recall a bright memory which concerns that good man, for on one particular day Lady Mary, Sir Thomas's wife, bade all the servants line up together in the great hall, saying she wished to speak to us on a matter of great importance. There were about twenty of us: cooks, housemaids, laundry maids, dairy maids, ostlers, footmen, butlers and valets, and you can be sure that on that day we were all looking our neatest and best. Milady stood halfway up the stairs where she could see everyone and told us that two very important personages were coming to the house and everything had to be faultless for their visit. The house was to be seen at the peak of perfection, the evening meal was to consist of the most rare and extravagant items, the musical entertainment to be the most delightful, the wines and sweetmeats the most delicious, and the whole household must work together to achieve this end.

'Every aspect of the house must be immaculate and we must fill our visitors with wonder,' said Lady Mary. 'We must show them that even in remote Oxfordshire we are able to be hospitable.' However, she went on to say, all this perfection had to be achieved as if by magic, for – apart from the waiting men who would serve the food – the servants were not to be seen going about their duties at any time. If we *were* seen we would be dismissed in an instant.

'Why should that be?' I asked one of the housemaids the following week as I flew between the innumerable jobs to be done before these fêted guests arrived. 'Why are we not to be seen?'

'It's not so much they must not see us,' she said, 'but we who must not see *them*.'

'Why then, who are they?'

'You goose,' she said, ''tis King Charles and Queen Henrietta who are coming. Did you not know that?'

I shook my head.

'But no one must know they are here, for there is money on their heads.'

I must have looked at her stupidly because she added, 'There's to be a war, haven't you heard? And it's to be called a Civil War – that is, 'twill not be fought with France or

Spain this time, but between ourselves and across our own lands. And the fight will be between those who are for the king, and those who are for parliament.'

'And we are for the king?' I asked.

'Of course! King Charles holds Sir Thomas as his friend and ally, and because of this the king and queen have chosen our house to say their goodbyes to each other before Queen Henrietta goes to France to sell her jewels.'

'Why is she doing that?' I had to ask, for I was as green as a sprout.

'To raise money for the king's cause,' she said, and then lowered her voice. 'But there are spies everywhere and no one is supposed to know of their visit.'

And so the house was made ready. The tapestries were taken out, beaten and re-hung, the wooden wainscoting hard-polished with beeswax, the portraits re-glazed, the mirrors gilded, and, on the day of their coming, fires were lit in all the rooms and the garden raided of every flower it possessed so that great blossoming arrangements stood on each coffer and table.

When the king arrived it was late afternoon and I was in my little room at the very top of the house. I looked out across the drive and remember thinking that if no one was supposed to know of his visit, then why had he arrived in a carriage and eight, for such an imposing retinue was almost unknown in Oxfordshire, and Sir Thomas himself only travelled in a carriage and four. The king's coach – what I could see of it from my window on high – was painted shiny red and purple and was very grand. The horses – all greys – had matching red and purple ribbons in their manes and tails, and the coachmen were in purple livery.

This retinue stopped at the marble-columned doorway and when the king emerged from his carriage he stood for a few moments looking across at the knot garden, then stretched out his arms and yawned. I was surprised at this and strangely thrilled, for until then I'd not thought that kings were real people who might suffer cramps and tiredness, but were somehow above all that. I had even childishly supposed that a king and queen, being so important, would be larger than ordinary people; perhaps as big as giants.

The king looked around him as if surveying the countryside over which he still had domain, and then gazed at the house and looked up . . . upwards . . . and saw me at my window staring at him in wonder. I waved to him and I *think* he smiled at me (I will always think so) and then Sir Thomas came down the steps of the house, bowed low and clasped his arm, and they disappeared inside. I did not see him again, but heard the musicians playing most of the night and, after his departure the next day, was given two sugared plums which had been left over from the banquet.

When he was beheaded last year I was very upset, and sorry for his wife and poor children, for it didn't seem at all proper to me that a king, who was God's chosen on Earth, should be put to death. I think many feel as I do, but we don't say so, for Cromwell has spies and the country is in his control now. Cromwell is not a bit like our tall and graceful king, who had elegant features and fine, curling hair and moustaches; Cromwell, they say, is short and stocky, with warts over his face, and I know I should be very frightened if I came face to face with him.

But not as frightened as I am now.

CHAPTER TWO

The morning of Saturday, 14th December 1650

At 106 High Street, Oxford, in a large, cold room above the shop of Mr Clarke the apothecary, stood a trestle table upon which rested a corpse in a coffin. The room was bare apart from this, although a meagre collection of twigs and a few dried-out cones had been placed in the fireplace ready for a fire to be lit. The only person in the room apart from the corpse was Robert Matthews, a scholar of New College, Oxford.

After attending the hanging in the prison yard and before arriving at the house of Mr Clarke, Robert had been to the Eagle and Child to take a tankard of strong beer, and then another, for what he had witnessed had fair turned his stomach.

He'd been to a public hanging before: two highwaymen who'd been hanged on a tree together, maggoty-headed, drunk and laughing, and an old man who was so befuddled in his wits that he hadn't known what way up he was, let alone what would happen when the noose tightened around his neck. The hanging of Anne Green had been different, for the girl had been young and comely. Shapely, too, as the crowd had seen, for after taking off her gown and cloak and bequeathing them to her mother, Mistress Green had faced the cold and driving rain wearing just her undershift. The thin cotton of this garment, soaked by the rain, clung against her breasts and defined their shape and the men in the crowd had hardly known what attitude to take, wanting to show a seriousness but having a lusty curiosity for such a well-shaped young body. Anne's mother, a care-worn creature, had come closer and tried to cover her with a blanket, but had been ordered away by the surly hangman so that he could go about his duties unhindered, leaving Anne Green to be hanged in the cold and rain with only a cotton undershift between her and nakedness.

Robert glanced over to the coffin, which had been placed next to the window so that its contents could derive the most benefit from the pale and unsatisfactory light of the morning. He was not generally squeamish, for he'd been a scholar at Oxford for a year, had seen drawn and quartered corpses as well as hangings and had also been present at amputations, but there had been something intensely depressing about the girl and her death; about the way that she'd stood, trembling, pathetic, in the prison yard, looking round in some awe at the attention she was receiving from the gathered crowd, her glance passing over them as she, perhaps, looked for a loved one.

And now her body was in that flimsy parish coffin that stood on the trestle table before him, her life blood hardly cool within her, for the hanging had been less than four hours ago. Had her soul yet departed? Robert wondered. Was her ethereal presence nearby – or had she, being a murderess, been consigned to Hell and was she already enduring its fires and eternal torments?

Even though he'd stopped at the tavern, Robert was first to arrive at the apothecary's house; the physicians weren't due for another half-hour or so. Being early he could, he knew, have taken the best place right beside the coffin. He could. But even as he told himself to move closer, get as near as he could to where the great men would be working so that he might garner every scrap of intelligence, he hung back, surveying the trestle at a distance whilst trying to warm his hands inside the sleeves of his black gown.

He thought of the coffin's contents. Why did he feel like this? What was he so apprehensive about? Anne Green couldn't hurt him. A girl like that, tremulous on the scaffold, trembling with cold, couldn't hurt a fly whether she was dead or alive.

But she *had* hurt someone, he thought with a start. She

was a murderess, had been found to be so by judge and jury, and thence had become one of the five hanged persons a year which the teaching establishments of Oxford were able to claim for dissection.

Robert forced himself to recall the scene early that morning when Anne had appeared from the confines of the gaol supported by two burly prison officials. She'd tried to cling, weeping and shaking, to her mother, but had been roughly pulled away by the hangman. 'I protest my innocence,' she'd whispered, and her words had been passed around the crowd. 'May God in his wisdom prove me innocent of the charges against me.'

Her speech was recorded by two pamphleteers who were standing beside the scaffold, endeavouring to write in the rain. The pamphlets, Robert knew, would be published on the morrow with many a linguistic flourish added and perhaps even a poem, together with an etching of Anne praying beside the scaffold steps and calling upon God's mercy. These would be best sellers – for cases such as this, tales of fornication and murder, could hardly be got off the printing press quickly enough.

He had watched, horrified yet fascinated, while Anne Green had climbed the ladder to the scaffold and the heavy noose had been placed around her neck. Her final words had been, 'May God convey me swiftly to Paradise,' but the last of these was hardly out of her mouth when the hangman shoved her off the ladder and that had been an end to her and her prayers. Some young men – her brothers, perhaps – had come out of the crowd and, weeping freely, hung on her legs in order to hasten her end, and one of them had lifted her body several times and pulled it down again with a sudden jerk, the sooner to break her neck and dispatch her out of her misery. After twenty minutes or so a sergeant-at-arms had climbed the ladder and pounded several times on her breast with the butt-end of a musket, using some considerable violence, in order to drive the last remaining breaths from her body. After thirty minutes, when she was observed to neither twitch, breathe nor move, her body had been cut down and pronounced dead by a prison official and a doctor.

So, Robert pondered, if Anne Green was neither bold nor fierce enough to hurt him in life, what was he frightened of now? Did he truly think that now, *dead*, she might have taken on a more frightening aspect? That as a wraith she was capable of doing him harm? But what was it that Dr Willis said about wraiths and ghosts? That they were nothing but creations of the imagination. That once the immortal spark was gone from someone, all that was left was a carcass.

* * *

Mr Clarke's maidservant, a girl named Martha with frizzy red hair and pale freckles, well-wrapped against the cold, came in and struck a tinder to light the fire, then began lighting tapers around the room. These, however, did little to dispel the gloom of the December day.

''Tis extreme cold,' she said to Robert, rubbing her hands up and down her arms to warm them, 'and the rain looks like turning to snow.'

'Tis the year's midnight, Robert thought to himself, and glanced up at the sky, which was leaden and streaked ugly yellow. For sure it would snow, and then perhaps it would seem more like Christmas – although Cromwell had already decreed that there should be no dancing, carousing or festooning of dwellings with greenery this year, but that people should simply offer up an extra prayer.

'A beggar died under St Clement's bridge of cold and hunger,' Martha went on. 'At least, he began to die in St Peter's parish, but the parishioners discovered him and carried him into St Clement's to breathe his last there and so to save St Peter's two shillin' for his burying!' She rolled her eyes to Heaven. 'That never used to happen with our king on the throne. If you ask me, people are acting meaner since Cromwell's been in charge. And now he's put a stop to mumming!' She seemed to check herself after saying this, looked over her shoulder and put her finger to her lips.

Robert smiled and made the same gesture back to her. It didn't do for a citizen to speak against Cromwell – or to speak in support of the royal line, either. Why, two fellows had been arrested in the Rainbow only last week for drinking a health to young Charles, the dead king's son and the contender for the throne.

Martha, obviously wanting to stop and gossip, pulled her shawl more tightly around her and nodded towards the coffin. 'Take yon girl, for instance. There's talk of whether she was truly guilty or not, or whether her employer had a hand in seeing that she was found so.'

Robert looked at her enquiringly, hoping she might say more, but she merely straightened up, pushed the hair out of her eyes and looked at him consideringly. 'You're here with the gent'men from the college to see the cutting?' she asked, and on Robert nodding, added pertly, 'Don't have much to say for yourself, do you?'

Robert swallowed nervously. She was pretty, but she was only Mr Clarke's servant and so of very little consequence. There was no call for him to be timorous. He could offer her a pleasantry, comment on the foul weather or wonder aloud where everyone else was. Nothing could be easier.

'W . . . w . . .' he began, and then cursed himself silently. *W* was one of his worst starts. He should have gone for a softer beginning. 'M . . . M . . . Mer . . .' he began again as Martha looked at him, head on one side. 'M . . . M . . .'

Realization spread across her face and she put her hand to her mouth and began giggling behind her fingers. 'Oh, I beg your pardon, sir,' she said. 'I didn't realize you were afflicted! But don't you strain yourself by trying to speak on my account. People say I talk enough for two anyway.'

Robert swallowed and nodded at the girl. This was what always happened, and it wasn't just with pretty girls, either. He'd grow out of it, his father had said. But what, he thought, if he didn't? What if he ended up a proper, qualified physician with a pronounced stammer? How would he attend to his patients and find out what was wrong with them? How was he going to be able to treat anyone if they giggled when he tried to ask what their symptoms were?

The church bells began tolling and Martha counted on her fingers, listening for the number of strikes. 'There! That's another soul hanged. A man this time. Pity *he's* not for the cutting instead of the young lass here.'

They both glanced to the coffin and Robert gave a sudden shiver as a forgotten memory stirred in him. A coffin . . . yes. He could see in his mind another coffin –

though not a parish box, but one fashioned from rich cherrywood with clasps and handles in gleaming brass. But who had it contained – and why had he suddenly remembered it with such vividness?

CHAPTER THREE

I search my mind for a prayer to help me through. *Though I walk through the valley of death, I will fear no evil.* But, oh, I'm in the valley of death now and I *do* fear it, for it seems to me that being shut alive in a box and put into the earth is the most cruel and terrible thing that can ever happen to anyone, for I swear I didn't do that wicked murder and God knows my innocence.

How could I be brought to this? Thinking on the answer to this last brings to mind my intention of recalling my life, and I let my mind dwell on the hated name of Geoffrey Reade.

Master Geoffrey came into the household when he was fourteen, about the time his father perished and Sir Thomas made him his heir. He was a big lad even then; as tall as a man, and strong and muscular, with a lot of fair curls and sandy eyelashes. I think about his appearance now, just briefly, and cannot say if he was handsome or not. I know I had thought so at first, for he had dark eyes like shiny brown conkers and they looked very well with his fair curls, but when I recall him now his face is clouded by my more recent thoughts of him and he appears ugly and defiled.

But I must put things straight in my mind; order my thoughts so that I don't lose my sanity. And the facts are these.

After Barton Manor was burned down in the war, the Reade household moved to the Great House at Dun's Tew, which is a village a short way off, having a manor house and farm held by Sir Thomas. The Great House at Dun's Tew is a very large and noble house, with many suitable and convenient offices, including a laundry and pressing room, a dairy, still room, brewhouse, salting room and ice house. All these rooms, however, meant more work for the servants, for whereas previously Lady Mary had elected to send out to have her pigs salted, her flower essences made or her ale brewed, now all these skills were done in the house. The manor-house grounds also contain a large dove-cote which houses 600 birds a-calling and a-cooing to each other day and night, two lakes well stocked with fish, a big kitchen garden and a farm which supplies milk and beef and mutton. With these the household is almost replete and hardly needs to look outside its gates for any other provision.

Things changed for all of us at Dun's Tew, however, for

with all the extra work there was not so much gaiety to be had. And 'twas not just this, but the fact that Sir Thomas and Milady were much altered by the deaths of Master Geoffrey's father and uncle and the destruction of Barton Manor in the war, and became stricter and more remote from us.

Master Geoffrey stayed with us but briefly when he was fourteen, for he was soon sent away to be a scholar in London. We were a busy household, however, for other members of the family came and went: aunts, cousins and grown-up nephews and nieces of Milady, so that there could be two or twenty of the family living there at any one time. We had a kindly old cook at first, Mrs Norman, who treated me like her own, but when she developed a toothache Sir Thomas said that she wasn't able to do her job properly and must go to the poorhouse. She was replaced by Mrs Williams, who didn't much like me, and she brought two other servants with her, and one of these was Susan, who was a housemaid and also her niece. Susan is my age but looks younger, for there's no shape to her and she's as thin and flat as a pressing board. Her face is flat, too, and scarce ever has any expression on it but a peevish one.

Susan and I started friendly enough, but then I did something which upset her and she has hardly given me a word since. This came about when we had two journeymen barbers call at the house to cut the hair of Sir Thomas and the other men of the household, and also to shave and bleed them. The younger of these fellows, Tobias, had a merry eye and we soon fell to laughing and joking together, and at the end of the day I offered to read his palm and tell his fortune, which Ma had taught me and which was merely a bit of fun. But telling palms meant I had to hold his hand, and Susan came upon me doing this at the scullery table and slammed out of the room in a temper, which I was very amazed at.

I excused myself from Tobias and went after her, catching up with her on the back stairs and asking her to hold a moment.

'Well might you ask me to hold a moment, Anne Green,' she said very crossly.

'What do you mean?'

'How dare you act the trollop with my suitor!'

'I did no such thing,' I said, astonished, for although Tobias was a merry fellow, he had a pink, round face and tiny eyes within it, and I didn't find him the least bit handsome.

'I saw you hand-holding, and looking at him so wanton!'

'I was telling his fortune – nothing more,' I protested. 'But I didn't know you were even acquainted with each other.'

'I knew him from my last position,' she said sullenly. 'We were friends whenever he came to the house and we . . . we had an understanding.'

'Oh,' I said, for I'd seen no signs of such a thing.

'But because you've been acting so shameless with your giggles and wanton ways, he's hardly spoken to me all day.'

'Well, I do beg pardon, I'm sure.'

''Tis too late now for the begging of pardons!'

'You should have told me that there was an arrangement between you.'

She went red. ''Tis not an arrangement as such . . .'

'I will go and ask his pardon this minute and tell him that I was sorry to have caused a falling out between you.'

This made her crosser than ever. 'You will not do any such thing!' she said, and as she spoke she gave me a hard pinch on my arm which later turned quite blue.

The next time Tobias and his brother called, about a month later, I stayed out of the way. Things did not go as Susan wished, however, for I heard from Jacob the footman that Tobias had hardly spoken a word to her. This was no surprise to me, for to my mind he was a skip-jack sort of fellow who would have a girl in every house. I tried to say this to Susan, but she wouldn't listen, and we were never friends again.

I get on well enough with the other servants, but Susan

was the girl I had to work beside and also share a room with, so the fact that we didn't speak was troublesome. I say work *beside*, for we were both housemaids and could be called upon for most kitchen duties, but over the last good while it had seemed to me that she'd been doing all the dainty work: the sugaring and the candying of flowers, the making of junkets and taffety tarts, the distilling of violets and the mending of lace collars, while I was responsible for the rest: the salting of the swine, the skinning of the eels and the morning ritual of emptying the chamber pots into the cesspit. The only cooking I'd been allowed to undertake of late was the making of calf's-head pie, and I believe that Mrs Williams only let me do this because she knew that such a business wouldn't be to my taste, and that rinsing out the brains of the creature and cutting out its tongue would certainly turn my stomach.

Mrs Williams is not what she seems, for the family think her an excellent and proficient cook, and indeed she always acts both humble and courteous when any of the family are about. They don't know her at other times, however, for I've marked many an occasion when she's been slatternly or dishonest. She takes her instruction from Mr Peakes, but they are birds of a feather flocking together and there are lewd goings-on between them, for I once surprised them in the brewhouse with his hand under her petticoats.

Not that I can think on that sort of matter whilst pretending to have the virtue of a maiden, however, for I must confess that I am that no longer. And here I think again about what happened concerning this and what it led to, and a dread comes over me. *Oh, let not me be alive and in the ground . . .*

Master Geoffrey. I must think now, carefully and truthfully, about whether I am to blame for anything of what came to pass.

When he was seventeen he came back from his school in the early summer and was much changed, for he had lost his boisterousness and adopted the manners and costume of a man. A *man*, I say, and not a gentleman, for I believe I know how they are supposed to behave and his manners were not conversant with one.

He began to flirt with me and to indulge in saucy conversation, which I supposed he had learned from his fellow scholars, and this led me into some confusion, for I was not sure of how to act in response. On the one hand I was mindful of the deep gulf between us – he the master and I the servant – but on the other hand there was something playful and pleasing about his manner towards me which was very appealing, especially as Mrs Williams and Susan were acting so cold.

By the strangest coincidence it was just about this time that I first became acquainted with John Taylor, a young and bluff fellow who was apprenticed to the blacksmith in the village.

When I picture John Taylor my heart contracts with sorrow, for if I'd not been so trusting, so easy to fool and so puffed up with my own vanity, then surely I wouldn't be lying here now recounting my downfall. If only I'd valued John for the good and decent man he was and not looked higher . . .

But I will think of him now, for he has a part to play in my story.

I had seen him in church before, and we had oft smiled at each other, but we began to be friends about the middle of May, on the occasion of one of our big wash days at the house. At these times Mrs Williams takes on extra girls and so my sister Jane had come over from Steeple Barton the night before. Jane is younger than me and still living at home, for she is very headstrong and not biddable enough to be a housemaid. She finds work enough to pay her way, however, for she tills the land in the spring and helps bring in the harvest, and is also able to turn her hand to glove-making, mending, sheep-minding or whatever else might be called for. That morning we had to rise at two to begin heating the water, but I was mighty pleased to have her beside me, and she and I talked the whole time of happy days at home as we washed and starched and blued the linen.

Our ma birthed six children, but two had died as babes before Jane and I were born, and our brothers, Jacob and William, were both working as grooms on a big estate in Banbury, which, being some distance away, meant we hardly saw them. Jane had news of who they were walking out with, however, and gossip from Steeple Barton, and although Mrs Williams frowned at our chatter she couldn't make much objection because we continued to work hard the whole time. Besides, she was pretty much occupied with the wash, not only but also with ensuring that the four extra girls were fed, but also with fiddling the accounts: marking down that we'd eaten meat for our dinner when we'd only had a dish of peas and some buttered eggs. (I found *this* out when I heard her whispering to Susan that she'd made two shillings on that week's accounting, so Susan was allowed to buy herself a ribband from the next pedlar who came to the door.)

When the first big sheets had been rinsed and wrung out hard, with Jane and I twisting them between us with all our strength, we folded them, loaded them in a basket and carried this between us to the drying ground – the orchard at the front of the manor house – to hang them on bushes to dry. This being done, we were about to go back to the house to begin again when there was a sudden yapping and yelping and two puppies came under the front gate and, before we could move, ran in and, jumping and clawing, pulled our sheets onto the ground.

Jane and I shouted and hastened to snatch up the puppies, and would have thrown them back over the hedge (which is not such a tall one) when John Taylor came running round the corner, still wearing his blacksmith's apron and as red in the face as if he'd been supping ale and pickled oysters all night in the Barley Mow.

'Ladies! My apologies!' he cried. 'I was minding them for my master and they got out of their kennel and ran amok!'

I didn't reply, for I was staring in dismay at two of our best linen sheets, which now lay on the ground with mud and paw prints all over the fancy embroidered 'R' lettering. John ran over to pick them up, but this made matters worse and I could not but scream when I saw him do it, for his hands were black with soot from the forge.

'Oh, no! A hundred pardons!' he said, looking down at the new marks with surprise and dismay. Jane gave a frightened shriek and I burst into tears, for I knew Mrs Williams would be furiously angry with us.

John Taylor picked up the puppies by their scruffs and

shook them, and seeing as Jane had joined me in weeping then, became flustered and confused and did not know how to deal with this situation at all. On questioning us, however, as to what he might do to make recompense, and discovering that it was Mrs Williams I was afeared of, he arranged to have the two sheets taken back to his ma's house and have her wash and blue them again, then return them to the bushes so that no one would be any the wiser.

This he did, and because of this we became good friends. Sometimes – when Mrs Williams was what she called checking stock with Mr Peakes in the cellar – I would go out on the excuse of collecting eggs from the dovecote and call over the hedge to him, or sit in the nearest apple tree and play jests (one morning I imitated a robin's call and had him looking in the branches for the bird), for his smithy stands just outside our gates and he was there most days a-striking and a-twisting iron, carrying on his blacksmith's trade.

Dearest John. I know now that a man must not be judged by his appearance and his means, but by how he treats others, and I wish with all my heart that I'd continued with him as my friend, and not been so stupid as to believe the lies which led to my downfall.

After I'd been sharing banter with John for some three weeks, and he'd made me a present of a little candlestick wrought in iron to go in the bedroom I shared with Susan, he came to ask Mr Peakes if he could have permission to walk back with me after church on a Sunday. As St Mary's, however, is less than a stone's throw from the back door of the manor house, John and I would extend this to walking around the village together and once, when we found the door of the Barley Mow open, we went in and he bought me a tankard of small beer. I was very happy that afternoon, for the men in there were giving the two of us smiling and knowing glances, and old Tom Hawkes once referred to me as John's sweetheart, which pleased us both very much (though we didn't say a word about it).

Although the rest of the household would sometimes tease me about John, calling him my beau and making me blush by saying that blacksmiths were strong and lusty men that it took a deal to satisfy, neither Mrs Williams nor Susan ever said a thing about our courtship, but always seemed busy when I returned from my walks with him; bent over an awkward bit of mending or deep in a whispered conversation. Even when John gave me the candlestick and, finding the stub of a candle, I lit it and stood it on our nest of drawers, Susan didn't say a word or even appear to notice it.

It was about June, then, that Master Geoffrey returned from his studies and began acting strangely. At first it was jokes – crude jokes, when I was alone with him (for he seemed to have an instinct as to where I was working in the house and come and seek me out). He would ask made-up riddles: what was the difference between a harlot and a pair of gloves? a beaver and a pock-marked whore? a prick and a burn? And of course I never knew what the answers were and so would repeat the question, which delighted him so immensely that he would ask me to say the words once again. It was then that I realized what was on his mind. And it was then that I should have stopped.

I did not, though, and from the riddles, which grew ever more outrageous and had me laughing and blushing, he moved on to pay me compliments. He'd say how rich my hair was, how blue my eyes, how shapely I appeared, how soft of skin.

'Dressed in silks and satins, Anne, you'd pass for a lady,' he'd say.

I'd try to be modest, but couldn't help being flattered. 'I'm sure I know my place, sir,' I'd reply.

'But wouldn't you like that, Anne?' he would persist. 'Wouldn't you like to wear a gown in the latest Paris fashion, and have servants of your own?'

'Yes, but I don't think that will happen, sir, so it's best not to even think about it.'

'And you could have jewels in your hair and a necklace

of sapphires to match your eyes! And it could all happen if you were a good and generous girl to me,' he'd say, and I'd get on with whatever I was supposed to be doing and pretend not to know what he was talking about.

One morning, when I was sent to the dovecote to collect eggs, matters advanced between us. Egg-collecting is one of my favourite duties, for it's softly dark in the dovecote, and very warm and close, and the cooing of the doves surrounds you so that you feel you're in a nest of your own. I began stretching up to the boxes to collect the eggs within reach and my trug was almost full when I heard a movement behind me and felt someone's hands on me in the darkness. I knew immediately that it must be Master Geoffrey and I gave a scream of fright that startled the doves so much that, with a frantic beating of wings, many flew up and away.

'Hush, Anne,' Master Geoffrey said, and he put one hand about my waist and the other on my bosom. I was very affrighted then, for until that time I might have persuaded myself that although his manner was a little too familiar, it was mere words and nothing that I couldn't manage. Now, though, I knew exactly where his mind was set.

'I have to take the eggs back for a syllabub, sir,' I said, and I lifted up my trug across my body and so shrugged off his hand.

'Just stay a little longer.' He spoke softly, pleadingly. 'You must call me Geoffrey.'

'I cannot!' I said, shocked.

'And I shall call you Annie.' He gave a little whistle, then sung under his breath, '*Annie Green, Annie Green, the prettiest girl I've ever seen.*'

I should have pulled away then (I have heard of maid-servants that are bold enough to slap a man – even a gentleman – for getting too familiar) but I didn't. Instead I am ashamed to say that I stayed to hear more.

'*Annie Green, Annie Green, the prettiest girl I've ever seen,*' he repeated. '*Annie Green, Annie Green, her kisses are like ho-ney.*'

And so saying, he knocked my basket to one side (causing about five little eggs to fall to the floor and be smashed) and placed his lips hard on mine.

I didn't move or push him away, for I was struck with astonishment and also – as I must be truthful at this time – took not a little pleasure at knowing that a young gentle-man of such standing should find me attractive.

When, after a moment, I did break away he spoke breathlessly. 'Annie. I could raise you in this world. Make you a lady!'

'I don't know what you mean, sir,' I said, very flustered.

'When my grandfather dies I will come into the

title and the estates and be able to do anything I like.'

'But how can that affect me, sir?'

'Why, it is then that I can marry you!'

I began to shake with giggles, for such a thing was so nonsensical that it could only be laughed at, but at the same time my heart was beating very fast. It was as if I could see a great treasure trunk opened before me full of gold, silver, glittering jewels and ropes of pearls, which could all be mine for the taking.

'I mean it, Annie,' he said earnestly. 'I have a strong desire for you. Oh, such a strong desire! If you let me have what I want, then as soon as I get my title I'll see that you rise in the world. You can become mistress of this house.'

I stopped giggling then, for I was dazzled by the dream of myself as Lady Anne of Dun's Tew, of commanding the staff, presiding over dances . . . and of docking the wages of Mrs Williams and Susan and dismissing them without a character.

But I was not so much of a jack pudding that I fell for this line of Master Geoffrey's straight away. Instead I looked into my basket and began to rearrange the eggs. 'Please don't trifle with the feelings of a poor servant girl, Master Geoffrey,' I said, and I whisked past him, knowing my way better than he in the darkness and moving before he could make a grab for me again.

I didn't say anything to anyone about this, for I had no one to tell, but I made up my mind I would inform Jane and Ma of it on my next afternoon off and see what they had to say.

The following Sunday after church I was, to my deep shame, pert with John Taylor, saying that I was bored with village life and might seek amusement elsewhere, perhaps in Oxford or even London. I was encouraged in doing this naughty thing after seeing Master Geoffrey, from his position in the first pew of the church, turn round and give me a look – *such* a look that when Susan saw it and realized it was for me, she gasped aloud. She never said a word to me after, though, and I know she regretted that gasp as much as I couldn't help but take pleasure in it.

Oh, but I should not have done, and I should not have suffered what came after. I should have stayed on the path of righteousness and kept my soul unsullied.

CHAPTER FOUR

As the notes of the tolling bell died away there came a
stamping and a shouting from outside and, skirting around
the coffin with as wide a margin as she could, Martha went
to the window and looked down. Walking across to join her,
Robert saw that this window overlooked the apothecary's
herb garden and was surrounded by a tall fence, against
which a collection of people had gathered. Shouts and loud
thuds could be heard as they banged their fists and cudgels
against the wooden gate through which the body of Anne
Green had lately been carried.

'See. They're trying to get in to rescue yon corpse!'
Martha said with some satisfaction. 'They want to give her
a Christian burial.'

'B . . . b . . . bu . . .' Robert tried. He wanted to say that
although dissection might seem unpalatable – even
barbaric – to the ordinary people, if bodies weren't cut up,
how was a physician to know how they functioned? How
could a surgeon work without knowing the best place to
make an incision for the stone, how to cut out a cancerous

growth with the minimum of blood loss or where to sever someone's gangrenous arm from their body?

'They're fearful angry; they don't like this a-cutting up of bodies,' Martha said.

'N . . . n . . .'

'An' it's always someone poor they cuts to pieces,' she went on before Robert could get out a full word. 'The *gentry* don't get flayed! Don't they ever commit murder? I vow they do!'

Robert gave up trying to speak and shrugged, thinking that what she said was true enough. The poor had precious few rights, and the bodies granted for dissection were always those of the lower classes; convicted felons whose families had neither the astuteness, nor the necessary means, to make a better offer to the hangman. Sometimes, there being no family to consider, the convicted man would sell himself to the dissectionist before he died and then drink away his body weight in ale and sack, for a corpse in good condition was worth a full two pounds. Three pounds, perhaps, if it was an exceptional one – as the fresh young corpse of Anne Green surely was.

There were noises in the hallway downstairs and Martha's face brightened. She set one last candle in a holder, lit it and went out. There was some laughter, a male voice was heard to say, 'I swear I'd swing for those freckles,

Martha!' and she replied, 'Go to, young master!' and came back into the room with her cheeks blushed pink. She was followed by two gowned scholars, both of whom were known to Robert by sight and reputation. First Edward Norreys from Christ Church College, followed by Christopher Wren from Wadham College. Wren, although only eighteen, was being hailed as something of a genius, for he already had the degree of Bachelor of Arts and was held in high esteem by the masters both for his remarkable intelligence and also for his most beautifully precise drawings of body parts. Both of them wished Robert a civil good morning, but he only nodded and smiled by way of reply, *G* being another of his bad letters.

'As you see, good sirs, I've made the room all ready for you,' Martha said with a curtsey, looking at Edward Norreys from under her lashes. Robert smiled to himself and, glancing at the fellow, could not but admire his style, for Norreys affected the curling lovelocks of a Cavalier and, with his old-style frilled shirts and plumed hat, cut a dashing figure. His study, it was said, was lined with oil paintings and silk hangings, and he even kept a harp in his bedroom so that, in times of anxiety, a musician could soothe him to sleep. 'If you need aught, let me know,' said Martha. 'Some refreshments later, perhaps. Some bread and cheese?'

'Thank you, Martha,' Wren said, and Norreys flicked

her a coin. She caught this and curtseyed again before she went out. Wren immediately drew closer to the coffin, looking at it keenly, as if he could already see the body through the wood.

Norreys stared out of the window. 'Bit of a crowd down there, but all seem to be of the lower classes – whores and harlots, pimps and panders.'

Just the dead girl's friends and relatives, Robert thought, good citizens all, and glancing once more at the coffin, he could almost feel some of their affection for her. If she was his, he probably wouldn't want her dissected either. He closed his eyes momentarily, trying to remember the other coffin he'd recalled but dimly. Had he seen it in a dream, perhaps? If so, it seemed an old and familiar dream, one that had perhaps recurred over the years – but, strangely, he couldn't recall it coming to mind in his waking hours before now.

'Perhaps peasants don't feel the cold,' Norreys mused. 'Seems there's snow about to fall but they're not going to be put off.'

Wren snorted. 'Are *you* going to be put off, Norreys? I trust you're not going to faint during the dissection this time.'

Norreys grinned. 'No, indeed. I've been steeling myself for this, and I cut up two toads and a dog last week in readiness. I would have had a cat, too, but another fellow got to it before me.'

'Y . . . you . . . you . . .' Robert began, and they turned to look at him. He wanted to say that Norreys might have had the body of the tramp under St Clement's Bridge if only he'd been quick enough. 'Y . . . you . . .' He could feel his colour rising; if only he could get a little further into the sentence he might be all right. 'Y . . . you . . . you . . .'

'Never mind, old chap,' Wren said after a moment. 'Must be blasted annoying.'

'Bad enough for us,' muttered Norreys and they all laughed, Robert included.

Martha came back in carrying a shovel of hot coals, threw these onto the fire, smiled at Norreys and went out again.

'I heard that it's damned cold in London,' Wren said, walking up and down the room in an effort to warm his feet, 'even worse than here. There's such a hard frost that the Thames has frozen over and hucksters' tents have been erected on it. The ice was so solid that a coach and six was driven right across it without so much as a creak being heard!'

Norreys drew a pen and bottle from inside his gown and frowned. 'But how are we supposed to make notes when the ink is frozen in the bottle?'

'Use a pencil!' Wren said, and he held up his tablet of drawing paper. With his other hand he took hold of his nose and pinched the end of it. 'And I tell you, good friends, I would rather have *this* weather for dissection than a stinking August.' The others nodded agreement and then all turned and looked once more towards the coffin, in which reposed the corpse of Anne Green, who would presently be sawn, dismembered, divided, cut, pared, sliced, peeled and flayed. No part of her would go untouched, unseen or unrecorded. Even her brain – Dr Willis having a keen interest in cerebral tissue – would be exposed to the world, weighed, analysed, pondered over, portrayed in charcoal and eventually preserved in vinegar.

Robert took a deep breath. This was his first dissection – such was the paucity of bodies and the demand to attend their cutting that a scholar had to take his turn. He'd seen a pair of feet dissected, it was true – for these had been the only parts of a hanged man that his tutor had been able to obtain – but these would not count towards his degree. For this he had to witness two complete dissections and also carry out two himself, as well as directly cure three maladies completely unaided.

'Did either of you see the despatching of this girl?' Wren asked. Robert nodded but he could not, of course, give his observations.

'I missed that, *and* the trial,' Wren went on. 'Was she hanged for murder or theft?'

Norreys shrugged. 'Who knows? All I heard was that she was a common trull who was servicing her employer's grandson.'

Wren asked who was her employer and was answered by Norreys that it was Sir Thomas Reade. 'Who is rumoured to be coming along to the dissection today,' he added.

Robert listened to this with interest. He'd heard of Sir Thomas Reade, of course, and had even glimpsed him at various meetings of the city fathers, for not only was he a Justice of the Peace, but also a wealthy and influential landowner with vast estates nearby.

'But his grandson – young Geoffrey – is only sixteen or seventeen,' Wren interposed.

'Aye,' said Norreys with a broad smile. 'I've heard it said that he's a forward youth.'

'And he's also Sir Thomas's heir and close to the old man's heart.'

Norreys nodded. 'So young Geoffrey could have had his pick of fair wenches – why should he bother with a grubby servant?' He shrugged and added, 'But I suppose she was near to hand.'

'And one never has to try too hard with them,' said

Wren. 'Though we should take care – that fellow Montgomery was expelled last year for attempting to ravish his housemaid, and now his father's cut off his allowance and he has to beg his bread at the Rainbow.'

'So we mustn't get caught with our hands in the maid's milkchurn . . .'

They laughed at this retort and Robert, eager to know more about Anne and the crime she'd committed but knowing the impossibility of asking, laughed with them, looking from one to the other and envying them the ease and precision of their speech. Once *he'd* spoken so, for he'd been told that before he was breeched he used to make the household laugh with his prodigious use of words he didn't fully understand the meaning of. Being an early reader and gaining access to his father's library, he'd memorized long passages of prose with which to entertain visitors. He couldn't remember those times now, though, those babbling, easy-speaking times, for something had happened in the intervening years which had thwarted his vocal cords, made them strangely unwilling to respond to his wishes, caused his words to choke in his throat and stutter on his tongue. Only in his head and in his reading was he lucid of speech – to the outside world he sounded like an idiot boy. And that, he thought, was what many people thought he was; even his father often lost patience and shouted at him, or tried to finish his sentences. His stepmother – well, she was tolerant enough but had more concern for her own eight younger children to bother with the one that she'd taken on merely to gain a husband.

The fire caught at last and the three students stood with their backs to it surveying the coffin.

'When we have done, will what remains of her be buried?' Norreys asked, nodding towards the corpse of Anne Green, and Robert looked at him gratefully, for this was what he'd wanted to know.

Wren nodded. 'If there's anything left then the family – that's probably them waiting outside – can claim it. Though often there's barely enough to make a dog's dinner.'

There was a sudden noise from the crowd outside, a long-drawn-out wail of despair which went on for several moments, and which Robert thought to himself could be Anne Green's mother, that bedraggled wretch of a woman who'd clung to Anne in the prison yard. None of the scholars commented on it, however, or showed that they'd even heard it.

CHAPTER FIVE

Summer continued, and I had some respite from Master Geoffrey's entreaties when he went to stay with his grandmother's family, who live in a great house called Brocket Hall in Hertfordshire. 'Twas immense hot for two of those weeks and we sweltered in the heat; indeed it became so very close that the cesspits stank day and night, the poultry died in their boxes and we maids took to leaving off our heavy aprons and sometimes even our day dresses and sitting about in our shifts. We would only do this latter thing when we were working in the sewing room, however, and there was no risk of being seen by the men.

One sultry afternoon Mrs Williams talked at the door with a fellow who'd come round the back of the house wanting to buy old pans and dishes. She told everyone that she'd sold him a battered dish for scrap, but I knew 'twas not battered at all, but a good pewter one with a lid, and what was more she'd hidden two live ducklings inside that could be fattened to sell. After doing this deal she, very pleased with herself, took half a bottle of claret and Mr Peakes, and went to the storeroom.

The other servants being employed elsewhere, I finished the work I was on, which was seaming pillowcases in the sewing room, and decided to go outside and find some flowers of feverfew to take with a little bread, for I had a headache because of the heat. But first I had to put on my day gown – a patched and worn affair which I had bought second-hand from the rag market in Woodstock – and I retrieved this from the back of my chair and threw it up and over my head.

Oh, what a shock I had then, for I hadn't even known Master Geoffrey was back, and he'd come up on me so stealthily that I hadn't heard his footsteps. 'I saw you in your undersmock,' he murmured, putting his arms around me, 'and you looked quite delightful. I have long missed you, Annie! I yearn to have you in my arms and in my bed, and to kiss you all over.'

I was at a disadvantage for I was caught up inside my gown, which had tight sleeves and a sewn-in petticoat, but did my best to wriggle out of the situation I found myself in. 'Please . . . sir,' I said. 'I am aware of the . . . the honour you do me . . . but . . .' As I was speaking I had somehow forced my hand down the wrong arm, and now had to endeavour to tug it out again. I managed this, but as I did so the thin, over-washed material of the bodice ripped across, making me cry out with vexation.

'Desist!' he said. 'I am mad for you, Annie, and I shall have you.'

'Please, sir!' I was all of a dither, as worried about the tearing of my day gown (for I had only one other) as about what might happen with Master Geoffrey.

'Don't they teach you that you should obey your master with singleness of heart?' he murmured, his face pressed against my neck. 'Don't you want to be raised in the world – to have a house and servants of your own?'

I did, of course I did, and just for a moment I hesitated and he pressed home his advantage and also pressed something else, which frightened me and – I must admit to it – excited me at the same time. 'I mean it, Annie,' he said, very hoarse. 'I shall love you and make you my own. I shall give you everything you want, and you can have a lady's maid and fine clothes and whatever your heart desires.' As he was speaking his hands were running frantically over my body, touching my private parts, and I thought to myself that it was not so very much, this thing he wanted. Not if, in exchange, I might become a lady. And I did not think about how stupid I was being, or how I would face John Taylor again, or what would happen if Master Geoffrey was telling me lies, but instead stopped struggling and allowed him to push me back against the linen press and have his way with me. And that was my first time. The first time with him and the first with anyone.

Immediately following this, I became horrified at my lewd behaviour, feeling myself only a step up from the meanest whores who, it is said, ply their trade under the bridges in Oxford. At this time, however, I truly believed that he cared for me and that I would sometime be mistress of the Great House at Dun's Tew, so made up my mind that I must at least act honourably towards John Taylor and discourage him. I felt sad about this, because our little conversations, our jestings, the clasping of our hands as we walked the lanes (for 'twas all innocence between us) had become a warm and happy part of my life. However, I knew that if I wished to obtain all that I'd been promised by Master Geoffrey, then for propriety's sake I must disassociate myself from John. Accordingly, the following Sunday after church when he came up and offered me his arm as usual, I didn't take it, but instead said very seriously that I had some important matter to speak to him about.

'Oh, so formal, Mistress Green!' he teased, and he took up my hand just the same and linked it through his. I noticed that his hands were scrubbed Sunday-pink and his nails were clean, and thought to myself that it must take no little effort every church day to get them like that, and all just for me. This touched me deeply, but also made me feel very sad.

I was conscious that, just ahead of us at the lych gate of the church, Sir Thomas, Lady Mary and Master Geoffrey were speaking to the Reverend Coxeter and perhaps congratulating him on the length of the sermon, which had almost reached two hours that day. As I glanced towards them, Master Geoffrey turned and looked straight at me. His glance took in John Taylor and was piercing, accusing, and I felt myself becoming flustered. What if he knew that John Taylor had been courting me? What if he thought he was *bedding* me? For certain then he would withdraw his promise to raise me in the world, and what I had endured through his attentions would all be for nothing.

'We must walk around to the back of the church,' I said to John quickly, 'and then I can tell you in private what I have to say.'

He looked at me, surprised at my tone, but we walked together to the old church garden. Some of the windows of the manor house look onto this space, but I was not apprehensive of being seen, for since our churchwarden was killed in the war it has become a mass of overgrown trees, tangled briars and weeds, and we were well hidden from anyone in the house who might have wished to spy on us.

We stopped by a fallen statue while I detached my Sunday-best tabby skirt from where it had got caught on a cage of brambles. Nearby I could hear children circling the church and singing, '*Well ploughed, well sowed, well harrowed, well mowed – and all safely carted to the barn!*' – for it would soon be harvest time and they were practising the songs.

'Is something wrong, Anne?' John asked.

'There is.' I moistened my lips but no words came, for I'd not thought of how I should order the matter. I looked around, seeking inspiration but finding none. 'It is just . . . just that I cannot allow our friendship to proceed any further,' I said after some moments. 'I hope you'll oblige me by your understanding.'

He smiled at me, looking almost relieved. 'You are jesting with me, sweeting!'

I shook my head. 'No, I'm not. I'm sorry for it, but I can no longer be your friend. I feel I must speak now, for already people are thinking of us as a couple.'

'And should they not?' he said, sounding bewildered. 'I thought you welcomed my friendship. I thought . . . well, I've thought all along that you and I made a fine pair.'

'That's as maybe,' I said, which is what Mrs Williams says and is to my mind meaningless and one of the most annoying phrases in the world.

'A fine pair,' he repeated warmly, 'and that in due course we'd—'

'Please don't say it!' I interrupted. ' 'Tis not to be.'

'But why ever not?'

I shook my head, then swished my hand through the weeds and, pulling up a long stem of chicory, began tugging at the blue petals. I felt horrid and wicked and ashamed of myself. Poor John, a kindly fellow, to be treated so when he'd done nothing wrong. To have scrubbed his black-smith's sooty hands and pared his nails for my sake, only to be cast aside.

'*He loves you, he loves you not*,' said John, taking the stem from me. 'Count with me, Anne. See whether or not I love you truly.'

I straight away dropped the stem, but he picked it up and began plucking the petals from one of the flowers. 'You see – *he loves you*,' he said as the last blue shape fluttered to the grass (although I think he had made it come out so). 'And you love me, do you not?'

'No, I do not, nor ever shall.' I swallowed through the dryness in my throat. 'And therefore I must allow you the freedom to seek a sweetheart elsewhere.'

He gave a hollow laugh, for there are precious few single girls in the village, and I suddenly thought of Susan, and how very much it would pain me if he began a courtship of her with her sullen little mouth and peevish face. And it was then that I realized that I didn't want anyone else to have him, that indeed I loved him, and that even though I might become the mistress of a great manor house, I was going to have to make many sacrifices along the way. And this was the first of them.

'There's more to this than I can tell,' he said, his voice low and gruff. 'Is it that you've met someone else?'

I hurriedly shook my head. 'No! Not at all.'

'No one has been acting improperly towards you, have they?' he asked harshly, his hands clenched into fists. 'For I would not hesitate to fight for you, Anne. Even if the fellow was twice my size.'

''Tis not that!' I said with haste.

'Could it be that you have your sights on someone higher placed than I?'

I shook my head, sweat standing on my brow, while the children's voices encircled us.

'For although I am only a jobbing blacksmith now, Joseph Parnell has promised to sell me the smithy when he is too old for the working of it, and that should be in only two years' time. And I already have a little money put aside for its purchase.'

''Tis not that,' I said, and without thinking I tugged at another weed, which turned out to be a nettle and stung me badly across my palm. ''Tis just that I . . . I do not love you.'

He was silent for a long while, then he said in a low voice, 'Hearing that fair breaks my heart.'

I did not reply and *could* not, for there seemed a lump in my throat as big as a dove's egg.

'Do you want me to go now?' he asked.

I nodded, but kept my face averted, for I could feel the tears brimming and feared that at any moment they would spill over. I had made my choice, though, done the deed, and knew there was nothing else for it. Even if I changed my mind, I was used goods now and no decent man would have me.

'I will say one more thing,' he said, his voice choked. 'I'm a proud man, but would not hesitate to have you back if you thought you'd made a mistake.'

'I have not,' I said, shaking my head, 'but I'm monstrous sorry if I've caused you pain.' With that I turned away from him, and a moment later heard the thud of his footsteps and the brambles scratching at his best serge breeches as he stalked off. I took up a piece of the chicory leaf and, bruising it, rubbed it across my palm where I'd been stung, as Ma used to do on our cuts and bruises when we were little, but it didn't help the pain in my heart and the knowledge that I'd caused a strong man, a burly black-smith, to have tears in his voice.

I stayed in the graveyard for some time, composing myself, and reflected that in some ways it was good that Susan and I didn't speak, because I wouldn't have to explain my discomposure to her or tell her that John Taylor and I were no longer walking out. I said nothing to anyone else, either, but the following day I asked young James, the boot boy, to take the candlestick that John had made me back to the smithy. James did so, and when I asked him what John Taylor had said, informed me that he'd said nothing, but had thrown the candlestick the length of the smithy then gone after it and kicked it into the street. That night I set my candle stub into a broken saucer again, and if Susan noticed that the candlestick was gone, she didn't say a word. I didn't say a word, either, about the fact that she'd bought a yellow silk ribband with the money from Mrs Williams and trimmed her cap with it, but I was pleased to see that the colour didn't suit her doughy complexion a bit.

How strange a fact it is, I think now, that I lie here not knowing whether I'm dead or alive, and instead of reflecting on the strangeness of the universe and the pity of my situation, think instead of such a petty and inconsequential matter as the colour of a silk ribband.

I try and clear my mind, and address again the matter of purgatory. If I'm there now, where are the fires that are supposed to burn and cleanse? I can feel nothing of them.

Maybe I've not reached the stage which has the fires. How long before I get to these, then, and what will that amount of heat be like?

Ah, I remember now! The Reverend Coxeter once told us that the fires would be unbearable, for only then would our sins be burned away. But how can they be unbearable, when there is no option but to bear them? And how long will I have to stay in them in order to burn away all *my* sins?

CHAPTER SIX

Five or six new fellows clattered noisily into the dissection room. Jacob's Coffee House had opened in the High Street only that week and several of them had been out celebrating the end of term with dishes of coffee and mulled wine, and were somewhat the worse for the experience.

'Move over there, you fellows!' came the shout from several of them.

'You've been warming your arses for long enough.'

'Give some others a chance!'

'Let the dogs see the rabbit!'

Robert and the others shifted to allow the newcomers to warm their hands at the fire and, once nominally heated, a hearty discussion ensued about the freshness and rarity of the corpse, the possible shapeliness of it, and who might be selected by the doctors to take notes or hand instruments.

As they settled into their positions, a young boy, servant to one of the doctors, arrived with a heavy leather bag full of dissection tools which he placed on the table.

'Don't you want to look at the corpse?' Norreys asked him, and jeered as the boy paled and ran.

One of the newcomers, a Christ Church man, began to dance a little jig, his gown swirling around him. As he danced, he sang a bawdy ditty from a new ballad sheet, a song about a girl with skin as pink as apricots who'd serviced half the young men in the town. As he sang the chorus he pointed towards the coffin in which Anne Green lay, thrusting his hips forward at the end of each line.

He finished and everyone roared with laughter, stamping on the rush-strewn floor and warming their feet at the same time. Robert laughed too, for he didn't want to be seen as a Bible-thumping Puritan, but he wished he hadn't. Wished he didn't think it necessary to laugh along with everyone else. Wished he could look solemn and explain why he was so – because he thought the poor girl had suffered enough without being ridiculed after her death.

'Was she hanged for whoredom, then?' one of the new-comers asked with interest. 'I thought she was a murderess.'

'Whore, murderess – much the same thing,' said the scholar who had sung the song. 'Though this one here is very pretty, by all accounts. *With a skin as pink as ap-ri-cots and her hair all tumbling down, o!*'

'Her skin won't be as pink as apricots now,' Wren

pointed out. 'For *rigor mortis* will have begun setting in and the blood will have faded back from the skin. She'll probably be yellow, tinged with blue.'

'Maybe she will, Wren, but that wouldn't be so pretty to sing about,' Norreys said.

Another of the newcomers shook his head decisively. 'Not *rigor mortis* already, surely, for 'tis scarcely four hours since she was cut down.'

'But 'tis damned cold and she may have *froze* into it!'

The crowd outside suddenly found their voices again and also began banging on the fence, their shouts penetrating the room. A man's cry carried clearly. 'Give us Anne's body!' he cried. 'Give her back!' and Robert felt certain that it was her brother, the fellow in a rough tweed coat who'd hung on Anne's legs.

Two of the scholars exchanged glances and then moved away from the window, fearing that they might be recognized and set upon by the mob later.

'Well, *rigor mortis* or not, I've heard that she's passing fair,' said Norreys. He tweaked the ear of one of the others. 'Here's your first chance to see a woman undressed, eh, young Wilton?'

Wilton, a gingery youth, blushed. ''Twill not be my first!' he protested, to some jeers from the others. 'I've seen my sister.'

'A sister doesn't count,' said Norreys. He grinned around at the others, encouraging them to take up the jest. 'And what's this we've heard about your mother moving into lodgings above yours, Wilton?' While the others jeered on cue, he added, 'Is it to see that you don't waste your money on card games and whores?'

'Whores?' came a bellow. 'He wouldn't know what way up to hold one!'

'My mother is merely staying here while visiting her sister,' Wilton said when the laughter died away.

'There'll be no chance of finding you with a naked woman in your rooms this term, then!'

Robert laughed along with everyone else, although he'd never had a naked woman in his rooms, either. Two weeks earlier, however, owing to a sudden determination to lose his virginity before his eighteenth birthday, he'd had carnal knowledge of one, and usefully enough, the whole procedure had taken place with hardly a word having to be exchanged. He'd spotted the woman – reasonably clean, with dyed-red hair and lustrous eyes – sitting on the parapet of Magdalen Bridge, which (so he'd been told) was one of the best places for the picking up of whores. He'd crossed the bridge very slowly, his stomach churning, and then walked back again, apprehensive about approaching her directly because a fellow in the Mathematics

Department had had his face slapped and a lawsuit filed for taking liberties with a woman who was merely selling mousetraps. This girl, however, was definitely a whore, because she'd asked him what he'd heard was the usual question – if he wanted to do business – and when he'd nodded she'd motioned with her head that they were to go under the bridge. Once enveloped in the muddy darkness there had been one awkward moment when she'd asked what he wanted and given him, at lightning speed, a selection of possible actions by her and their various costs. He had not endeavoured to speak, though, nor question the amounts, but instead had taken some coins from his pocket and pressed them into her palm. She'd counted these carefully, then deftly carried out what he presumed was the course of action covered by such an amount. So swift was this procedure, unfortunately, that all he could recall afterwards was a swift realignment of body parts, a blur of movement and a couple of seconds of delighted surprise – which led him to wonder whether the sum paid always equalled the pleasure obtained, and, if he was to pay double next time, whether twice the pleasure would ensue.

But thanks be to whores, he thought, for otherwise, being so afflicted, how could he even speak to a respectable girl, let alone get to know one well enough to perform that other matter?

* * *

Minutes passed and a new man was shown into the room by Martha: a young surgeon by the name of Nathaniel Frisk who was attending the dissection as an observer. He was well thought of by the physicians (despite being merely a surgeon and thus affiliated with the barbers) and attended as many dissections as possible.

A bench was brought into the room and placed behind the first row of standing students, so that those who came later would have a better view of what was going on. As the scholars regrouped themselves there was a shout from the fellow at the door that they were to look lively, and after a moment the imposing figure of Sir William Petty, wearing a sleeveless scarlet cloak over a black gown, came into the room carrying rolled-up charts and a heavy medical book. He removed his tasselled cap and nodded to the assembled scholars, and they in turn returned a deep and respectful bow, for Dr Petty, who was twenty-seven years old, was quite a favourite. Tall and good-looking, with goose-grey eyes under brows that were thick and straight, he was, as every student there knew, marvellously good-natured and affable. He had studied at Amsterdam, Utrecht and Paris with men who were prime exponents of experimental science, had been made a Fellow of Brasenose College and was tipped to become Professor of Anatomy. His only perceivable fault was a tendency to overeat.

He was followed into the room by John Clarke, the tall and weedy apothecary whose house they were in, lauded throughout Oxford as a fine chemist and expert beekeeper, and he and Dr Petty immediately engaged in close conversation. Two minutes later Sir Thomas Reade appeared wearing the outfit of a country gentleman: a heavy wool surcoat over checked breeches and high leather boots. He carried himself with some pomposity, and his red-blue nose and cheeks were crisscrossed in a mesh of broken veins.

Sir Thomas ignored the scholars but bowed in turn to Petty and Clarke (a shorter bow to Clarke, Robert noticed, for after all he was not a gentleman, but merely a shopkeeper) and they returned the courtesy.

'Are you here as a Justice of the Peace, Sir Thomas?' Mr Clarke asked politely. 'Or is dissection one of your interests?'

Sir Thomas shook his head. 'The crime committed by this . . . this *woman* here affected my household,' he said stoutly. 'I am here to see justice done and this unsavoury job carried through to its end.'

'The corpse, one Anne Green, was a serving maid in Sir Thomas's house in the village of Dun's Tew,' Mr Clarke explained to Dr Petty.

Sir Thomas nodded brusquely. 'She was. And I rue the

day I ever took in, for she proved to be nothing but a scheming whore.'

'Tsk . . . tsk,' murmured Dr Petty.

'And a murderess to boot,' Sir Thomas added for good measure.

Dr Petty raised his eyebrows. 'She is dead now, Sir Thomas, so perhaps you may speak of her more appropriately.'

But Sir Thomas merely made a short harrumphing noise and turned away, pushing himself into the first row of the scholars and making them shuffle along to accommodate him. Robert, feeling himself dwarfed by such a hefty bulk of tweed, turned and climbed onto the bench behind, leaving Sir Thomas standing foursquare in front of the coffin with his arms folded across his chest. Sometimes, Robert thought, a gentleman would faint on seeing a corpse dissected for the first time, but he didn't think Sir Thomas was going to suffer this indignity.

Dr Petty removed his academic gowns of black and scarlet, donned a bloodied white butcher's apron and rolled up his sleeves. 'Doctor Willis will be with us shortly,' he said, 'but in the meantime we will remove the corpse and place her on the table ready to begin work.' He gestured to the nearest two youths, who happened to be Robert and Christopher Wren. 'If you please, gentlemen.'

Robert exchanged startled glances with Wren and, without saying a word, one went to the foot of the coffin and one to the head. They made a contrasting pair: Wren dark and stocky, Robert slight and very fair. Together, they lifted the wooden lid to expose the body of Anne Green to the dissectionists.

CHAPTER SEVEN

Some strange thing has happened. I am still here, un-moving in the darkness, but the quality of this dark has changed and is now a strange black-grey. It is lighter, some-how. Am I ascending to Heaven? No, that cannot be, for surely I've not yet been lying here hundreds upon hundreds of years – the length of time we were told purgatory would last. But perhaps that number of years *has* passed. Perhaps an age goes in a moment when you're in purgatory. There's no way that I can tell. Perhaps all these incidents with John Taylor and with Master Geoffrey happened a thousand years hence. Oh, but I fear that they did not, for I feel them close by me and inside my head as if they would overwhelm me.

But as I cannot know if my endurance is about to end or only beginning, I will return to my story and recall how when, about the end of the summer, Master Geoffrey went back to continue his schooling, it was a mighty relief to me. I did not welcome his attentions, nor ever had done, and felt that once he was out of the way I might not be constantly anxious and affrighted by what was going on between him and myself, and what might happen to me if Sir Thomas found out that we'd bedded. I would lose my job for certain, but worse than this, I feared the punishments I would have to suffer for being discovered to be of loose morals.

I sinned in all six times.

The first act in the sewing room was over very quickly, leaving me to ponder afterwards how such a small and strange act could be so very important and worth so much. Wonder of wonders, that doing such a thing could obtain me riches! But I must have been distempered in my mind at the start of it, for I'd stupidly supposed that when Master Geoffrey said he'd reward me if I let him have his way, then I'd only have to allow him to do it once. That first time, however, far from cooling his passions, seemed to inflame them, and soon he was trailing me around the house with his blood hot and his mind set on a jolt with me again.

The second time was a week after the first and happened in the dairy in the following circumstances. Lady Mary, who'd been laid low with some malady or other, had given word through her lady's maid that she had a fancy for a milk junket. Mrs Williams and Susan being out at the weekly market in Stapleton, I thought to make this – or at least begin it – so had gone over to the farm in order to obtain milk fresh from the goat. I put a pan of it on the fire to warm, added rennet to make it curdle, then poured it into a dish to cool. I'd scraped a sugar loaf upon it and was about to grind cinnamon for the top when the far door leading from the kitchen garden opened and Master Geoffrey came through. Straight away I hid myself behind a pillar and waited, quiet as a mouse, for him to go out again.

But he was looking for me – and indeed had found me, for a flounce of my skirt was showing round the pillar.

'I see you and have got you now, Annie Green!' he said, and then with no more ado he fell on me, endeavouring to get one hand down my bodice and the other into my petticoats.

'Please, sir!' I said, backing away from him, for although the dairy was at the far end of the kitchen, it was only separated from it by a tiled wall and anyone might have seen us. 'Please, sir, don't!'

'Go to it with your please sirs!' he said. 'For you are as hot as I and don't deny it!'

'If anyone sees . . .'

'If anyone sees, they will not dare say a word, for they know I am to be master of this house. And a master's wishes must always be obeyed!'

I wriggled away from him and darted round the table, and indeed 'twould have been almost farcical to see us, with me circling the room and him in hot pursuit after me, already fumbling with his breeches.

'Annie. Annie! Don't you want to be mistress here?' he asked. 'Have you already forgotten everything that will be yours?'

I didn't say anything, for I'd only just realized how green I'd been, and that the act would probably have to be endured many more times in order to keep him satisfied. And whenever would I get what I'd been promised? For although Sir Thomas was upwards of sixty years of age, he was in robust good health and did not seem about to roll over and leave his lands and fortune to Master Geoffrey just yet. Wondering then what would become of me, I began to wish with all my heart that I'd not submitted in the first place, for we are told often enough when we begin work as maids that gentlemen may try and take advantage of us, and we must therefore be sober in our discourse and never gay, so that they may not think we are open to levity. But – oh, stupid girl – I'd certainly been frivolous with Master Geoffrey, and from this he'd deduced that I'd be persuaded to lie with him.

I stopped going mulberry bush around the table then, knowing that my protests were useless, and stood against the cold stone sink, waiting. I only counted to seven before the act was finished, but sometime during this my dish of junket got knocked onto the floor, so that when Mrs Williams returned and heard of Lady Mary's request she scolded me for not having had the intelligence to obtain the goat's milk from the farm earlier.

The third act happened in Master Geoffrey's bed early one day when I'd been sent in with his morning washing water. He has a stately bedroom, with ewer and basin of silver, two mirror glasses and a vast feather bed with four posts hung about with costly drapes. I don't usually carry the washing water around and hoped that he'd be asleep – indeed, I removed my shoes and tiptoed across the thick carpet in bare feet – but he seemed to know it was me for his eyes sprang open the moment I set down the jug on the washstand. He was out of bed in an instant, took five strides across the room, picked me up, threw me onto the bed and drew the curtains around us. When George, his manservant, came in a moment after, he told him he must leave and come back in ten minutes.

Of course, George didn't know who was behind the drapes with Master Geoffrey, but he knew *someone* was, and spread the tale downstairs. The servants began gossiping and speculating and, knowing it must be someone in the household, before long had all deduced it was me, although I never admitted it. Instead of teasing me, though, as they had about John Taylor, they were quite mean in their comments. Mr Peakes said that no good would come of it; Mrs Williams, pinch-faced, said that that was as maybe but I needn't start putting on airs and graces; another said that when a youth was Master Geoffrey's age, *anyone* would do, and one of the menservants winked at me and said that if there was aught left over, could he have a share. I began to feel bitterly ashamed of our association, which I could not even justify by saying that I loved him – for which emotion, I believe, many such similar sins of the flesh might be forgiven.

The fourth time with Master Geoffrey was over by the carp lake. I'd cast the fishing nets onto the water and only then discovered, by him coming up behind me quietly over the thick grass, that he'd followed me out there. Seeing I was less than willing to do what he wanted, he tickled me until I was doubled up with mirth and pushed me into some myrtle bushes, swearing on his mother's life that he was devoted to me and would make me mistress of all I could see. Indeed, he said he would make me queen of England, too, if he'd been able.

The fifth time – oh God, I swear I didn't want this or encourage it in any way – the fifth was in the churchyard amid the tombstones, where the ground swarms with souls and spirits and surely 'tis a profanity to carry out such an act.

The churchyard. Am I there now, still breathing but under the earth? Oh, I pray not, for I swear that nothing I have ever done in my life has been wicked enough for that fate to befall me.

The sixth and final time was on the stairs in the dark, after he'd worn me down and made me weary enough to scream at his continual pleadings, saying things such as he loved me entirely and couldn't carry on without easement, and that I was being cruel and selfish to deny him this one thing before he went back to school. It was over very quickly, but I felt so bad afterwards that I told him I didn't wish to go on with it when he returned, no matter what he might promise. He insisted, however, that it must and would continue in December, when he returned to the house.

'For seeing as you've lost your maidenhead, how does it matter whether you do it more with me or not?' he asked.

I had looked at him, not discerning his meaning.

'For your maidenhead won't come back if you were to keep your legs together until the day you died!'

I turned away from these crude words, not wanting to hear more.

'And a fellow will always know, even though some jades try and fake their virginity. So you may as well be nice to me, Annie, for I am your only hope.' He ran his hand up my arm and tucked it inside the puffed sleeve of my blouse, pressing his fingers into me hard. ''Twould not be a clever idea to turn your back on me now.'

'You may be right, sir, but indeed I wish you had not started it!' I burst out.

'*I* start it?' he asked. 'I wouldn't say that was the case, Annie. It could be said that you led me on with your giggles and blushes and your unseeming language.'

My face flamed, but I had no reply to this, and knew that aught I said would be twisted and shaped to suit his own ends. I began to cry and after looking at me askance for a moment – for we were still on the stairs and mighty close to the door of his mother's room – he pulled five silver shillings out of his pocket and pressed them into my hand.

'Here. Stop your women's weeping,' he said, 'and buy yourself something fancy to wear with this.'

I'd stared at the money in awe and not a little consternation, for five shillings was the most money I'd seen altogether in my life, and near equal to my year's wages after my livery is taken off.

'You must spend it on something splendid to wear,' he said, 'for when I raise you up you'll be required to dress as a great lady, and this can be the start of your wardrobe.'

I'm ashamed to say that these silver coins were enough to turn my head and I took them from him, knowing they were enough to buy me a very handsome gown or three second-hand ones, and after this we parted and said no more. I was most happy and relieved to see him go back to school, however, and I resolved that, come what may, I would not succumb on his return.

There being nowhere in Dun's Tew to spend such an amount of money, on my afternoon off (with Mrs Williams being busy in the cellars with Mr Peakes) I took a ride on one of the carts going into nearby Woodstock, which is a fine and fashionable town. Here in a shop on the high street I purchased – not a gown, but a most beautiful bodice embroidered all over with silver thread and embellished with pearls. I did not have a skirt to match it in beauty – nor indeed any occasion to ever wear such an item of clothing – but I kept it wrapped in tissue paper under my mattress and sometimes took it out and looked at it. I told no one about it, for I'd already been chastised by Mrs Williams for wearing a red petticoat on a Sunday and knew the bodice wasn't a suitable thing for a maidservant to own.

I never wore it. The last time I saw it was in prison, when I handed it over to Ma and then went to meet the hangman.

Chapter Eight

As the coffin lid was removed, Robert found his hands were shaking and he was unable to look directly upon the corpse, although for what reason he couldn't say. Perhaps he feared that the girl might have taken on a terrible aspect; her face contorted and her eyes starting from their sockets. Perhaps it was that he didn't know whether she lay in the coffin in her undersmock, or naked – and that if the latter, he feared that the sight of her might induce some fellows to sniggering, or to make lewd jokes which even the presence of Dr Petty might not prevent. But then, he reasoned, Dr Petty would probably cut her clothes off before they started the dissection, so that sooner or later she *would* be naked before them all. And more than that, for very soon they would not just see her skin, but her flesh, her muscles, her bones and her very heart. No, he thought, it was something to do with that other coffin; the one that remained elusive to him. Despite being recalled but hazily, it was a matter of such high sensitivity that it almost hurt him to think of it.

But when Robert finally forced himself to look at the body of Anne Green (for they had not bothered to dignify her corpse by wrapping it in a shroud) he saw nothing too gruesome. The girl was still wearing the stained and wet undersmock that she'd been hanged in, and although her hair was in damp strands, her face, streaked with tears and dirt, seemed in repose. The flesh of her arms and legs was creamy white – as white as the cheap cloth that lined the coffin – her face was somewhat pink – due to, perhaps, the breaking of blood vessels – and the only strange and jarring aspect of her appearance was that the great knotted rope by which she had been throttled was still around her neck.

As the lid was placed on the floor there was a movement from the scholars as they craned and peered into the coffin.

'You may remove the corpse,' Dr Petty said.

Robert swallowed the bile which had risen in his throat, thinking to himself that strong beer too early in the morning should be left to more experienced constitutions.

'You take the top half,' Wren instructed him.

Robert nodded, then slid his hands under the dead girl's shoulders. As they lifted her, the hangman's rope slid towards the floor, jerking her neck and, for a ghoulish moment, making it look as if her head had nodded.

'She moved!' Norreys said in alarm, and there was a collective gasp from the assembled students. Dr Petty, engaged in unrolling a chart, glanced over and smiled slightly. 'My dear boys,' he said, 'I can assure you that she did not move. She has been dead these three hours and more.'

'She is certainly dead,' another confirmed with a slightly nervous laugh. 'She hung over half an hour on the scaffold. And her family swung on her legs to hurry her end.'

'Until the gaoler told them to stop for fear the rope would break!' another added.

Robert opened his mouth to add something of his own and then thought better of it. No matter, for one of the scholars had seen the same thing and was speaking his lines. 'I saw someone batter her breast with the butt of a musket to help her on her way.'

Dr Petty nodded. 'She is undeniably not of this world.' An ironic smile played across his lips. 'Even now she may be knocking at the door of Heaven.'

Dr Petty's charts had been unrolled and put up on the wall behind him. One depicted a skeleton, every bone down to the smallest precisely labelled; another showed the muscles in the body, red and livid; the final one was a depiction of a human head, the front of its skull removed to show an approximate replication of the whorls, cavities and coils within the crater of the brain.

The dissection tools – knives, saws, gimlets and pliers, brass probes, pincers, curved needles, syringes, long-handled scissors and a range of small knives with blades as sharp as razors – had been removed from the bag and stood at the ready and, although a corpse was not expected to bleed much, wadding had been provided and there was a pile of it at the head of the table. As a further precaution, Martha came in with a pail full of sawdust from a nearby coffin maker's and threw handfuls of it onto the floor. She stole a quick look at the corpse as she went out, shuddered dramatically and then looked at Norreys to see if he was looking at *her*.

The crowd outside in the High Street seemed quieter now, for a small detachment of soldiers had arrived and were rough-handling anyone foolhardy enough to get too close to the fence. Robert wondered to himself how Anne's mother – and her younger sister, had it been, who'd been near her in the prison yard? – were faring. Were they still waiting out there in the sleet with the others, or had they gone home to mourn?

As Dr Petty and Mr Clarke conversed in low tones about who was going to take responsibility for which part of the body and in which order, the scholars either spoke amongst themselves or just stood and stared first at the charts and then at Anne Green, trying to work out the positioning of some of her interior organs for themselves. Robert stared too, and fell into a kind of reverie in the staring, trying to remember more details of that other coffin and who'd been lying inside it.

The fellow next in line, young Wilton, nudged him, making him start. 'Were you at her trial?' he asked.

Robert shook his head and Wilton directed his speech behind his hand so that Sir Thomas could not overhear. 'The whole business of the trial and hanging was a strange one,' he confided. 'And an unjust one, it seems to me.'

Robert looked at him with interest, for he knew Wilton to be a fellow who took a deep interest in the politics of the day. It was rumoured, too, that he'd kept faith with the Levellers at one time, until the last rebel band of these fellows had been rounded up in Burford the previous year and their leaders shot.

'*He*' – Wilton nodded towards Sir Thomas and lowered his voice – 'had too big a hand in it.'

Robert was anxious to know more but, curling his lip with frustration, knew that it was well-nigh impossible for him to pose the question.

Sir Thomas suddenly spoke up, his voice brusque and impatient. 'Will it be *much* longer to wait? When are you going to start the business?'

Dr Petty pulled out a pocket watch, which the students

regarded with a deal of interest. 'We are waiting for Doctor Willis. I believe he had an important laboratory experiment already booked for this morning.'

Robert wondered what this was and if it might be something innovative and radical – like the recently posited notion from Dr Willis that catarrh did not pass into the nostrils from the brain, as had always been presumed. He thought of the experiment *he* was currently running which involved a chicken and a constant supply of eggs, the contents of which were examined and logged a certain number of days after they'd been laid. The chicken, whom he'd named Scarlett on account of her red feathers, lived in his lodgings with him, ate scraps and provided him with quite congenial company for, to his surprise, Robert had found that he could talk to her almost normally and with rarely a stammer. She was let out into the yard every morning for regular liaisons with a rooster and so far no one had noticed her presence in his room; although the students were forbidden to keep greyhounds, ferrets or hawks, a chicken appeared to be beyond this censure.

At last there came the sound of footsteps hurrying along the passageway and Martha's voice was heard to say, 'Just along here, sir, if you would be so kind,' and a moment later Dr Thomas Willis came into the room wearing a wool cloak which he discarded at the door to reveal a stained black gown. Although not as charming a figure as Dr Petty – for Dr Willis was plain, stocky and had hair as red and bristly as a pig's – his intense intelligence, plus his avowed intention to unlock the secrets of man's mind, was causing immense interest in his work both with the Oxford students and in the scientific world generally. He had recently written a treatise on sadness, saying, controversially, that it was a complicated distemper of the brain and heart and not a melancholic humour at all. Robert felt himself lucky to be at Oxford with such a brilliant physician, and profoundly pleased that his first dissection would be conducted by him and Dr Petty.

'Good morning, gentlemen, and my apologies for keeping you waiting,' Dr Willis said, bowing to all corners of the room.

He went directly to the cadaver and walked up and down the table surveying it with a keen eye. He slouched as he walked, Robert noted, and did not have the bearing of a gentleman or person of quality. He was certainly a gentleman in the true meaning of the word, however, for he had long treated the poor without payment.

'This is the murderess? She seems a very mild one.' He caught up one of Anne Green's hands and examined it. 'She was a housemaid?'

'Indeed,' said Mr Clarke, the apothecary. 'A housemaid

who was found guilty of murder, although she maintained she was . . .' He suddenly caught the eye of Sir Thomas and his voice faded away.

'*She* maintained?' enquired Sir Thomas. 'Are you saying, sir, that the word of a whoring housemaid should be taken above that of judge and jury? Are you saying that the law of the land was not properly implemented and that twelve good and educated men were wrong in their judgement of her?'

Everyone in the room waited for a response.

'Not exactly,' Mr Clarke said at last. 'It's just that she maintained her innocence until the end and—'

'Have you ever known a convicted felon who did *not* proclaim his innocence?' demanded Sir Thomas.

Mr Clarke, who could be easily cowed, shook his head.

'Fortunately, we are not concerned with the girl's guilt or innocence now,' interrupted Dr Petty, 'for it's obviously too late to discuss the finer points of the accusation. No, we are here with the express wish of improving our understanding of the functioning of the human body.'

'Then I suggest you get on with it!' said Sir Thomas.

'Indeed,' said Dr Willis, 'for the fresher the body, the more we shall learn.'

Sir Thomas nodded. 'Quite. Quite. For even without the murder charge, the new laws state that fornication may be an offence punishable by death, so the jade has got what she deserved.'

'But who was it that she fornicated with?' Wilton whispered to Robert. 'Should he not also be culpable?'

Robert, although rather startled by this thought, found himself nodding.

'There has been some skulduggery here, you may depend on it . . .' said Wilton.

Dr Willis picked up a whalebone rod tipped with silver and twirled it in his hand. 'Shall I begin?'

'If only you would, sir!' came from Sir Thomas.

Dr Willis moved forward and, watched closely by everyone in the room, tapped the tip of the rod against Anne Green's breastbone.

A tiny sound escaped from her mouth.

Only Robert heard it. At least, he *thought* he'd heard a faint noise, like the far end of a sigh, but with the press of people around couldn't be perfectly sure of the direction from which it had come.

He stared at Anne Green, pale, silent and immobile on the table; her life force extinguished over four hours ago and dead as a flitch of bacon. Of course he hadn't heard anything. But . . . He suddenly shivered so violently that Wilton gave him a concerned look. He saw, clearer than before, that *other* coffin. He saw another corpse, a young woman about the same age as Anne but tranquil and serene in her death, wearing a white ruffled nightgown, with dark curls showing at each side of a white cap. There were candles standing at the corners of the table, and the room was perfumed with a sweet, high scent. Incense, he thought to himself – although it had been banned from churches and it was a while since he'd last smelled its fragrance.

Wilton pinched his arm gently. 'You've gone as pale as a wraith, good fellow. Are you all right?'

Robert formed his mouth into a *yes* and nodded his thanks. He pulled himself back from his reverie, paid attention to Dr Willis.

'I am about to dissect the corpse of a woman,' the doctor said. 'She appears in good condition and was not suffering from any malady before her demise. With your permission, gentlemen' – he made a flourish towards Petty and Clarke – 'I intend to make the first incision under her ribs and then open up her chest cavity to reveal her heart.'

But as Dr Petty and Mr Clarke bowed back, another sound came from Anne: a faint raddling noise. It was a noise, Robert thought, more generally made by a corpse breathing its last than by one which had been pronounced dead some hours ago.

This time, most of the room heard it, and, although the medical men did not seem unduly disturbed, the scholars gasped and Sir Thomas Reade took a step backwards, looking affrighted.

''Tis nothing, merely the last breath she took, coming back from her lungs,' Dr Petty said calmly. 'I have heard such a thing before.'

'I know what to do,' said a fellow standing on the bench, and he did no more than jump up onto the table and stamp down hard on Anne's chest and neck. 'That will see her off!'

Robert and several other of the scholars gave a cry at this violation and Dr Willis ordered him off the table. 'That was unnecessarily brutal and could have harmed our specimen,' he said brusquely.

The fellow looked put out. 'I merely sought to help, sir.'

'Then please do not,' came the stern reply.

Dr Petty picked up Anne's hand and felt around her wrist. 'There is no pulse here and no signs of life,' he said. 'I suggest we proceed with the dissection forthwith.'

CHAPTER NINE

Such a pain! Such a pain of a sudden came upon me, as if someone had hammered across my breasts and my neck and my ribcage. And there was no way of expressing it nor of screaming out with the agony of it, so I had to contain it within me and thus it seemed so much worse.

For a time (a moment? a hundred years? a thousand?) I could not think of anything but this pain, and then gradually, very gradually, it diminished. When it allowed thought to come in, I wondered to myself if it was the beginning of the torment I would have to endure to enable me to progress through purgatory. In that case, perhaps, I should not fear it, but welcome it. It did not continue, however, and once the first agony was gone I felt nothing but a dull ache right across my body.

At the start of the cider-making season I had my afternoon off and walked home to see my ma, only to discover a terrible thing; a thing which I had felt in my heart but which I had pushed away as being too dreadful to consider.

My home village is about three miles from Dun's Tew. 'Tis a pleasant enough walk over fields and cart tracks, though 'tis a sadness to see the ruins of Barton Manor, now all tumbled and near disappeared under brambles and briars. On crossing the common I met some of my old neighbours picking the last blackberries, and also saw our family's two sheep, Bramble and Bracken, grazing peacefully near where the maypole used to stand. All was just as I remembered and how I like to recall it – although since I've been working for the Reades I've never visited my home without thinking of how small it is, and how humble. And indeed I thought it then, for 'tis but two rooms, one down and one up – this latter reached by a ladder – also an outhouse where the chickens live and are joined in winter by the sheep and, if Pa has had the money to buy one that year, a pig. There's no glass in the cottage windows up or down, and the wooden shutters which do their best to keep the wind out also serve to keep out the light, so in winter it's necessary to burn a tallow candle even by day. In our downstairs room there's a wide hearth containing a spit, cauldron and kettle, but there's no bread oven, so Ma buys her daily loaf at the baker's, and is thereby allowed to take her own pies and pasties along to be baked in his big oven. The room has not much furniture but is homely, with two benches, a table and an oak coffer that stores linen and trenchers and so on. 'Tis passing sufficient, for there's only Jane living at home now, and Pa is not often there, nor ever has been, for he labours long on the land and takes on extra work whenever he can and for whatever master. 'Tis long been his ambition to buy a cow and they don't come cheap.

I know that Ma is not a clever woman when it comes to book learning, for she has not had a day's schooling in her life and cannot even write her name, but there are certain things she knows about, for I'd not been long inside the door before she put aside the piece of lace she was making and looked me over carefully.

'You're pale of face and have rings about your eyes,' she said. 'Are you with child?'

I protested that I was not, even though I had not seen my courses for nigh on two months.

'Are you sure, Anne?'

I began shaking my head but she said, 'I know the signs! Have you lain with a man? Don't lie to your own ma!'

Of course, I did no more than burst into tears and say I had.

'Is it your young man's? Is it John Taylor the blacksmith's child?' she asked, for I'd not been home since the beginning of July, and at that time John and I had been seeing each other regularly.

I didn't reply to this, for I was too ashamed, and she must have felt pity for me for she reached over and took my hand. 'Well, you needn't take on so,' she said, 'for many girls anticipate their wedding and you'll not be the first. We can fix a date now and when the child comes early no one will say a word.'

I still did not speak.

'Take heart, my girl,' she said, squeezing my hand. ''Tis not what I wanted for you, but the Reverend Belchard will be sure to marry you, and we'll give you a little feasting.' She paused. 'Where will you live, though? What sort of dwelling can John Taylor provide?'

I continued weeping. 'I've not set eyes on John Taylor these past three months,' I said between sobs, which was not exactly true, for I knew exactly where he stood in church and out of the corner of my eye had oft seen his strong and upright figure, face resolutely turned to the front with never a glance towards our servants' pew at the back of the church. I would stare at what I could see of his head, note how his black hair touched his Sunday-white collar and went in a soft curl over it, and wish with all my heart that I had not given in to Master Geoffrey.

Ma gasped. ''Tis *not* John Taylor's child?'

I shook my head.

She dropped the hand that she'd been holding so

tenderly. 'Someone *else* is the father? Oh, Anne, for shame! Who have you been a-tumbling with?'

I cried harder then and couldn't look at her, indeed was so very much ashamed of myself that eventually she relented and, putting her arms around me, promised that she wouldn't reproach or chastise me if I told her the truth. So I told her about Master Geoffrey and how he'd been so friendly and easy with me, how he'd promised me gold and silver and the tenure of the Great House at Dun's Tew if only I'd lie with him, and how eventually I'd been persuaded.

She shook her head with each sentence I uttered. 'Oh, Anne, you simple girl,' she'd said, sighing again and again. 'To think you'd fall for such false and honeyed words.'

'But he's a gentleman,' I protested, 'and I thought 'twould be well enough to trust him.'

'The gent'men are the very worst.' She looked at me closely then slipped her hand onto my belly to feel the shape of it. 'When did this start with him?'

'About the first hay-making,' I said, for I remembered that there had been revels in the village on that very hot summer day and morris men dancing on the green, despite the new rulings that there should not be such tomfoolery.

'And when did your terms cease?'

I told her and she calculated that I was perhaps three months with child.

'But all is not lost if we're quick,' she said, 'for there are certain plants and herbs which are said to bring down a woman's courses.' She stood up and took her shawl. 'We must visit the cunning woman at once and find out which they are.'

I should have been back at Dun's Tew by five o'clock, for Lady Mary was having a musical evening and there was a deal of dainty sweetmeats to be prepared for it, but we decided that, my absence being noticed, I would say that Ma had been taken ill and that I'd had to stay with her until Jane came home. Ma and I then went together to the cunning woman's hut, which was on the common close to the Hoarstones where the goblins were said to be buried, and for the excursion I wore Ma's old cloak and had a shawl close around my head, for I didn't want to be recognized going to such a place.

There are those who say that the cunning woman is a witch, but I don't think she is; she's just an old and bent woman who lives with three cats and a lame fox. Her hovel has a stamped-earth floor and a hole in the roof to let the smoke out, and she has only one chair and a planked bed to call her own – and surely if she was a witch the Devil would have seen to it that she had more comfortable surroundings? She said that I was with child for sure, and, judging from my tear-streaked face that I did not wish to be, picked hyssop and sage from the profusion of herbs which grew around her cottage in tangled skeins and pounded them together in some agrimony water, which she then bottled. She told me not to take more than a scanty amount of the hyssop mixture – a bare spoonful at a time – for the herb's powers were so strong that an overdose could lead to poisoning. She also gave me a jar containing a decoction of the leaves and berries of the bay tree, saying that I should add this to a bowl of hot water and sit in it, for it was a sure remedy for a woman in distress. Ma paid by giving her a chicken and promising another come Christmas, and this seemed to satisfy her.

I went home with Ma and she boiled some water over the fire and sat me in a washing bowl containing the bay mixture (for of course there was not the privacy to do such a thing at Dun's Tew) and Jane, who'd been out earning money bird-scaring in the fields, came in by and by and laughed heartily to see me placed so in the bowl. I explained to her what was wrong, however, and swore her to secrecy – for Jane loves to gossip – and she went very quiet and serious. She listened to my tale but did not seem impressed with aught that Master Geoffrey had promised any more than Ma had been, even though I said I'd have taken care to raise them, too, and had Jane to come and live with me as my companion. As I said these words, however, they struck me as false, mere fancies, and I wondered how I ever could have believed them.

I sat in the water nigh on an hour but nothing happened, not so much as a gripe or a cramp, and afterwards I dressed myself and took the hyssop cordial back to Dun's Tew to drink before I went to bed. The cunning woman had said that I should stay close within the house after taking it and be prepared with clean rags to stem the flow that would ensue, so I couldn't sleep that night for worrying about how bad the pains would be and how I'd keep the matter a secret from Susan. In the event, however, nothing happened and my undersheet stayed unsullied.

In the morning I took another spoonful of the cordial, and then another, but was scared to take more because of what she'd said of its power. When, a day later, it was clear that it wasn't going to work, I poured the rest of the mixture away and threw the bottle into the midden.

I was at a loss then, and thought about getting a message to Ma but decided against it, not wanting to make her anxious. After more sleepless nights I decided that there was nothing else for it but to carry on as usual and, should my condition begin to show, lace my stomacher and bodice tighter and try to be patient until Master Geoffrey came back at the beginning of December. He would know what to do, I told myself. He was young, but had been educated to deal with such vexing questions, so would surely order things and see that everything was well. Perhaps he'd pay for me to go away and give birth in London, where no one knew me and where, I'd heard, these matters were not of such great import. Lodgings there would not be difficult to obtain, and the child and I could live there quietly until such time as my seducer came into his inheritance. For at that time part of me still believed that he that had caused my condition would support and help me and that I wouldn't be left to bear things on my own.

Thinking on the future, then, I felt that all was not lost, and tried to put the matter to the back of my mind, content in the fact that Master Geoffrey was away and that I would not have to put up with his pleadings and fumblings for the next good while.

As I related, people speak of the cunning woman of Steeple Barton as being of the Devil's brood, but I'm sure she's not. A more powerful witch, to my mind, is Mrs Williams, for in the days following my visit home it seemed to me that she was always speaking of childbirth and pregnancy – seemingly innocently, but with one eye upon me to ascertain my reactions.

One tale in particular was a favourite: the story of Sara Freeman, a girl from a nearby village who'd died after a long and painful struggle to give birth, for it was said that her bones were too narrow to let the child pass through. She'd been buried swiftly, for it was a hot summer, and then a day later a village crone, walking through the churchyard, had heard the faint crying of a baby. Thinking it a ghost, she'd fled the place, but then some sense had come to her and she'd returned and reported to the cleric what she'd heard. He, already fearing some catastrophe, called for the gravediggers and the coffin was exhumed. When the lid of it was lifted, it was found to contain not only Sara Freeman, but also the body of an infant, newly born and newly dead, for it seemed that, after burial, Sara had remained alive long enough to give birth.

Mrs Williams would oft recall her, and tell of another woman some years before who was said to have been delivered of thirty rabbits, and yet another whose path had been crossed by a hare and who'd borne a child with a hare-shotten lip. She told of women who'd died in travail, and those who'd birthed children conjoined, and said that there was no telling what ill creatures might be born now, for

God was grievously displeased with those who'd beheaded His anointed king and this was His way of punishing them.

'The world is turned on its head now,' she said one morning when I was at the salting table in the scullery. 'And all we can do is pray that God will not choose to punish us for Cromwell's great sin.'

I didn't speak, for I was concentrating on the job I was doing, which was rubbing salts into a dead sow's skin, the better to preserve the animal over winter. 'Twas nasty work, for every so often the salt crystals would get into a cut or graze on my hands and cause me to wince.

'So we must carry out our jobs quietly and well in the station in which He has placed us,' she went on piously.

'Amen,' Susan said. She was chopping hard-boiled eggs for a garnish, and I knew without looking that she had a righteous expression on her flat face.

Mrs Williams, who had been looking at me critically for some moments, suddenly said, 'Anne, you have dressed your hair differently this morning.'

'Have I?' I asked, although I knew full well that I had set my cap further back on my head and waved the front part of my hair so that it fell curly around my ears. I had seen girls in Woodstock with their hair dressed so, and it had looked very well on them.

'Indeed you have. And the manner of your hair is not in

keeping with your position, for haven't I just been saying that it does not behove us to try and rise above our stations?'

'You have.' I nodded. The smell of the eggs rose and hit me, and I was hard pressed not to gag at it.

'Well, then, 'tis not seemly that you should primp yourself up. You're only a housemaid and should know your place.'

I didn't reply, but noticed Susan glancing at me slyly to see how I was taking this.

'The fashioning of your hair that way makes you look saucy and impudent,' went on Mrs Williams, 'so go upstairs now, comb out your curls and put your cap on your head properly.'

I went, of course, and was glad to get out of the egg-stinking room for a moment and rinse the salt off my hands, but I made sure that I pulled in my stomach and held myself tall as I walked out.

I didn't know how much they knew or if they'd guessed my condition, but, aware that Susan had taken to staring at me as I undressed, I always turned away from her before taking off my gown at night. What I feared most was that it would be detected that I was with child before Master Geoffrey came back, for then I would be dismissed of an instant. And how would I then be able to approach him?

With Mrs Williams's awful tales fresh in my mind I began to dream horrid dreams of giving birth to an infant that had no limbs, or of not delivering a child at all, but a silver fish. I never ever had a dream where the babe that was born to me was pink and plump and full of contentment. Not ever.

I began to pray fervently that God would forgive me my fornication and bless me so that I'd see my courses again. Even as I prayed, however, I knew it to be unlikely that He would forgive, especially as, wickedly, I now looked for any weakness or ill-health in Sir Thomas, signs that he was going to die so that Master Geoffrey might all the sooner come into his inheritance. I saw none, however, and he continued as robust as ever.

About a month after I'd been to the cunning woman, I had a dreadful shock, and as they say that a shock can cause a woman to miscarry a child I did hope for this, may God forgive me, but it was not to be.

This shock started off as seeming to be favourable news, for we heard that Master Geoffrey was returning briefly to Dun's Tew. This was earlier than I'd anticipated and would enable me to see him the sooner, tell him of the trouble I was in and have his help in the resolving of it. When, however, we were at our dinner in the servants' hall two days before he arrived, Mrs Williams landed a substantial game pie on the table and said, 'Well, whatever news do you think I heard this morning from Lady Mary?'

Everyone looked at her, for we all loved hearing intimacies about the Reades, whom we knew just as well as – and indeed saw more of than – our own families.

When she had everyone's attention she went on, 'There is to be a special supper on Saturday for Master Geoffrey, and what do you think the family are celebrating?'

Thinking it was his birthday or that he'd had some success with his studies, I didn't pay much attention, but looked eagerly towards the great pie, for after two days of sickness I was suddenly hungry.

'It concerns a certain young lady,' Mrs Williams said, cutting through the pastry.

A young lady. I heard these words and at first didn't register their import.

'Such a lovely young lady, so Lady Mary told me,' Mrs Williams went on, deftly slicing and scooping. 'Sixteen years old and heiress to a vast fortune.'

I went cold. As cold and still as I am now, for I knew then where this story was heading.

'Oh!' everyone cried, and, 'There's a fine thing!'

'Are she and Master Geoffrey already betrothed?' someone asked.

'They are! Or will be after the supper,' Mrs Williams

said, 'for Lady Mary told me that a ring has been made from her own mother's emeralds. Spiced peas, Mr Peakes?'

Several of the servants around the table began exclaiming and I knew some were looking at me, but I said nothing. I looked down at my plate and did no more than begin to count the number of peas I could see there. *Betrothed*. Oh, then I was truly lost.

We were all served. We lowered our heads and Mr Peakes said grace.

Susan trilled, 'Amen!' merrily, then said, 'Oh, how romantic! Master Geoffrey and – what's the lucky girl's name?'

'Her name is Clementine,' said Mrs Williams. 'Miss Clementine de Millet.'

'When do you suppose they met? And when did he propose?'

''Tis of no account when they met,' said Jacob dourly, 'for most likely this agreement was forged between the families years back. 'Tis always that way for the nobility.'

'Not so,' corrected Mrs Williams. 'Lady Mary said 'twas a love match.'

'Aye. He loves her money,' said Jacob.

I burst out with a snort of laughter that was close to tears, and everyone turned to look at me and then looked away. I knew how their tongues would wag the moment I disappeared to bed.

''Tis excellent news for Master Geoffrey and the family. Don't you think so, Anne?' Mrs Williams asked.

I opened my mouth and then shut it again. I swallowed. I began re-counting the peas. I knew I mustn't speak in case I began to cry and then everyone would guess my secret.

I didn't care about him. Oh, not a jot. I didn't care if he was betrothed to someone named Clementine, I didn't even care that I wasn't going to be the lady of the Great House at Dun's Tew. What I *did* care about was what was growing in my belly and what would happen to me when everyone found out.

'Our Master Geoffrey!' said Susan, more animated than I'd ever seen her. 'There'll be young ladies aplenty who'll be breaking their hearts when they hear the news that he's betrothed.'

'That's as maybe,' said Mrs Williams, 'but they'd be silly young ladies if they believed that he'd ever choose one of nobility who was not favoured by his family.'

'Indeed!' chimed Susan.

Mrs Williams looked at me slyly. 'Not eating your pie, Anne? Don't say you've lost your appetite again.'

'No, indeed not,' I stuttered, and I forced down the

food and sat there for the rest of the meal, and again as we sat mending stockings after, (while such a deal of bibble-babble ensued about when the wedding might be and whether we might be issued with new gloves and caps for the occasion) whilst pretending all the time that nothing they said was of the least concern to me.

That night I had my worst dream ever, for I dreamed that I was trying to birth a monstrous strange tree with twisting, gnarled branches which snaked outside my body and tried to strangle me. I knew that I was dreaming, but was no less terrified for this, and tried my utmost to make myself wake up, pinching my arms with my fingers and trying to force my eyelids open. When I eventually did wake, there were tears wet on my cheeks and my heart was beating as fast as that of a dove.

It was still dark in our room, and I whispered across to Susan to ask if it was near morning, for I was fair desperate to speak to someone – even her – and be reassured that I was safe and back in the real world. She didn't reply, though, just turned sharply in her bed with a squeak of the springs and an angry, impatient noise, which I took to mean that she was cross that I'd woken her with my tossing and turning.

Remembering that dream, that night, and how I'd

endeavoured to force open my eyelids and wake, I try to exert a mighty effort of will to do the same thing again. If I managed it once, then why can't I do it now?

Because, reason tells me, I was merely asleep then.

Now I am dead.

But I try nonetheless, and make a vow that I will keep on trying until the darkness comes to consume me . . .

CHAPTER TEN

Robert's heart thumped. That other corpse. *Had* it been a dream? It seemed very like one, a dream that faded as fast as recalled, drifting away as cloudy and insubstantial as chimney smoke. He closed his eyes. *Think*. A room, a coffin, and he there – yes, he – but as a child. Where had he been, though? And who had been the corpse?

Dr Willis glanced about the room. Two years older than Dr Petty, he was, it seemed, going to take overall charge of proceedings. 'I agree we should begin,' he said. 'Would you take the pointer,' he said, handing the rod to Norreys, 'and as I cut into the corpse and locate the organs, point to where they are on the wall chart for the benefit of those unsure as to their whereabouts.'

Norreys gave a short bow and went to the other side of the coffin, where he smirked round at the rest of the scholars, pleased to have been chosen. Robert nodded back to him, thinking that Wilton was more *his* sort of fellow; someone one might go for a row on the river with, play cards, down ale or snort over the latest college gossip. But why would a fellow like Wilton bother with someone like *him*? Someone who couldn't speak properly?

'Wren will make accurate drawings for us,' Dr Petty said, and Wren, who had taken up his drawing block, nodded.

The scholars pressed together, closer to the coffin, and Robert found himself so close to Sir Thomas Reade that he was able to feel the big man twitching, fuming and bristling with impatience. But they could not begin cutting yet, Robert knew, for it was usual for the leading doctor to quote some words from Galen before he started opening the body, making the claim that human dissection might be unpalatable to some, but was essential for the furtherance of medical knowledge.

Accordingly, with silence in the room apart from the bronchial breathing of Sir Thomas and an occasional shout from the crowd outside, Dr Willis began: 'The work of this day is to open the way into the Practice of Anatomy and into the knowledge of man's body . . . to care and ease the distempers that befall it, and to show proud man that his most mysterious and complicated energy is nothing to the compounded mysteries within the very fabric of man itself.'

The scholars nodded sagely, taking in every word, for Dr Willis was an excellent orator. As the doctor spoke, Robert stared at the woman lying before them, trying to forget her similarity to another figure at another time. He tried instead to see her as a practice piece, someone who hadn't actually lived at all, so that the shock of seeing her being dissected wouldn't be too great. He'd been told what to expect and braced himself for that first cut to the stomach, the stink of viscera, the tumbling out of the guts and the strange and unnatural sight and sounds of a body's inner organs being pulled into sight. To think that this woman, just a few hours ago, had been a cogent human being: living, breathing, loving, hating. To think that those arms had clasped her mother in a final embrace, that that mouth had spoken, bidding goodbye to the cold world, and her eyes had looked upon the same doleful scene of hangman, tree and noose as he had. Now she was just a lump of flesh.

So where had the part that animated Anne Green gone? Was it still somewhere inside her body, or had it left for a higher plane? If still within, would it escape and fly away when the doctors cut into her? Should the window be opened for such a purpose?

Robert had seen four deaths at close quarters, although in three of these he'd arrived just too late and the only duty he'd been able to perform was the closing of the corpse's eyelids. At no time, however, had he noticed any sort of spirit or presence coming from the body. Was the soul something one could see? he wondered.

There was a sudden and very loud scream from outside. 'I want to see her!' came the cry, and it was repeated twice more.

Robert started. I want to see her. *I want to see her.*

And of a sudden he remembered. Twenty big steps down the stairs at home, on each step a word, a comforting echo in his head.

I

want

to

see

her.

These words, repeated four times each, had brought him down to stand outside the drawing room of their home in Somerset.

I want to see her. He knew that, as a small child, he'd been saying these words a long time. Two or three days or more, for he could almost taste them in his mouth.

I want to see her. But he wasn't allowed to see her because she was busy. She was resting. She had gone out. She was sleeping.

His mother.

I want to see her. He'd slept at last with those words on his lips and in his head, and woken when the rest of the household was asleep. And then he'd climbed out of the bed he shared with his nurse and come down the stairs to the library, somehow knowing – had he heard a whisper of it during the day? – that this was where she would be.

He remembered now the way he'd pushed open the door to flickering candlelight and a table bearing a cherry-wood coffin. He recalled now how tall wax candles had stood guarding each corner of the coffin, their light reflected off its polished wood. He saw again the mirror, portraits and tapestries hung about with black muslin, and his family's coat of arms, proud with lions and castles, draped across the window shutters.

He remembered staring at the scene for some moments, trying to work out in his child's mind what it meant, and then pulling a chair across the room and clambering onto the table to see inside the box.

And *there* was the woman he'd so much wanted to see. There was his mother, her face ivory, her dark hair waxed, wearing a gown and cap of frothy white lace. Her eyes were closed and her hands clasped at her breast with a Bible placed between them.

I want to see her! He gave an involuntary gasp and was aware of Dr Petty turning to glance at him, no doubt think-ing he was feeling nervous about the dissection.

My father hadn't told me, he thought. When I asked to see her they said she was busy at some household task or she was resting or was unwell, and all the time she was a dead corpse in her coffin.

And when he'd discovered her that night in the drawing room, what had happened next? He couldn't quite say. He remembered touching her cheek and feeling it cold, and then could remember no more. But later, when he was a little older and had asked his father about the death of his mother, he'd been told that she'd died abroad, of a strange disease. And then, very quickly, his father had married again and his mother had been talked of no more.

Dr Willis's voice rose again. 'For the end of anatomy is knowledge of each part, why it exists, for what purpose is it necessary and what is its use.'

Sir Thomas Reade sighed impatiently and Wilton looked at Robert and raised his eyebrows. Robert gave a slight smile back.

They had thought to protect him, perhaps. Or maybe his stepmother was jealous of the other woman's memory. He would ask his father again, now. Ask him for the truth about the death of his mother.

Taking a deep breath, he tried to dismiss the matter from his mind, and concentrated once more upon the body of Anne Green, his eyes taking in each part of her. From healthy peasant stock, she was of excellent stature, her legs long, her body shapely, her arms full and muscular. Her face was fair: a curved, full-lipped mouth, a straight nose, her eyelids now a translucent violet. She was fair and she was dead – and her death had been untimely. She should, he thought, have lived to provide a home for a man who loved her, and together they should have bred a houseful of milk-maids and sheep farmers. Her last view should not have been of a hangman, but of her cottage fire sixty years hence. Those eyes of hers should have finally closed on—

Those eyes! As Robert's gaze rested on Anne's face, his reverie ceased and he became shocked and fearful, for her eyelids had seemed to flicker, as if there was life still within her body.

Shaken, his belly churning, he stared at Anne's face until his gaze blurred – but did not see movement again. Should he say something? He almost smiled at this. What was the point of trying to speak? By the time he got his words out, Anne would be in pieces.

Robert nudged Wilton to signal to him that he should look at Anne. If there *was* anything amiss, let him see it too. Only let someone else see it! Robert frowned, nodded, indicated with little jerky movements what he was trying to convey, but Wilton just looked at him, puzzled, and then turned back to gaze reverently at the two doctors.

There!

Robert had seen the eye movement again; the smallest

flicker from within her, like a hearth fire which, although put out hours before, suddenly gleams within with a tiny glow-worm brightness. Oh, he must speak! He must speak now or die in the attempt. Before he could consider its delivery, the word, '*Sir!*' came from him fast as the retort of a gun. Every eye in the room turned to stare at him and his face grew hot.

'What is it?' Dr Willis asked, frowning.

Dr Petty looked at Robert with concern. 'Are you feeling unwell?'

Robert shook his head. He stepped forward and pointed to Anne's face; to her left eyelid. 'Moo . . . moo . . .'

There was a snigger behind him. He heard a voice say in a low voice, ''Tis Buttercup the cow,' and there was some stifled laughter.

'*Movement?*' Dr Petty asked. 'Eye movement?'

Robert nodded violently, then pointed at his face and made twitching movements with his own eyelid much more violent than those Anne had made. 'Eye moo . . . moo . . . movement!' he confirmed.

There was an outbreak of gasps around the room, a chorus of disbelief. Robert heard the singing scholar say, 'The fellow's been drinking for sure.'

'Either that or he's fallen in love with the wench and doesn't want her touched,' came the reply.

There was a bellow from Sir Thomas Reade. 'What is all this? What the Devil's happening now?'

'Has anyone got a hand mirror?' Dr Petty asked. He turned to Mr Clarke. 'You, sir?'

The apothecary shook his head. 'There's one in the hall but 'tis the size of a door.'

Dr Petty bent over Anne. 'We need a small mirror to see if she breathes.'

'There's not such an object in the house!'

Dr Willis edged around the table, frowning down at the corpse and bending low over her. 'There's no need for any mirror, surely. Her chest is not rising and falling. She does *not* breathe.'

Mr Clarke took up Anne's limp wrist and felt around it. 'No. And I feel no pulse,' he said. He replaced her arm and it fell off the table, dangling, blue-tinged white.

The three doctors turned to look at Robert, who was still watching Anne's face intently. 'Are you absolutely sure you saw movement?' Dr Willis asked.

Robert nodded vehemently, his mouth forming the word *yes* several times over. Already he was doubting himself, though. Had he imagined it? It was snowing quite hard now and the light in the room was thin and pale; the beer he'd taken had been strong and he'd stayed up late the night before writing detailed comments and suppositions concerning the contents of Scarlett's last eggs. Perhaps, feeling pity for the girl . . . perhaps, being confused with the wonder of that other, newly remembered, corpse, he'd allowed himself to be deceived into thinking there were still signs of life within Anne Green.

'Carry on, sir!' Sir Thomas bellowed.

'This is most unusual. But we must be completely sure,' said Dr Petty, sounding a trace distracted.

'Just put her out of her misery!' said Sir Thomas. He gestured to the fellow who had stamped on Anne's chest before. 'Come,' he invited, nodding towards the corpse. 'Help her on her way again. Let's dispel any argument about whether she lives or no.'

The fellow hesitated. His lips twitched nervously as he looked to the physicians for guidance.

'No, you will not!' Dr Willis said. 'Stay where you are, sir!'

'Doctor Willis and I are in charge of this dissection,' Dr Petty reminded Sir Thomas.

'So what in the Devil's name is the matter with all of you?' Sir Thomas asked, exasperated. 'She has departed this mortal life. She was dead when she was cut down and she's dead still. Just look at her lying there and then tell me there's any doubt about it.'

The students shuffled their feet, exchanging alarmed

and excited glances. What a thing it would be to talk about later, Robert thought. To discuss – if one was able – with fellow scholars in taverns.

'You doctors make a fuss about obtaining cadavers to cut up, and now you've got one, you're treating it with as much reverence as you would your own mother!' Sir Thomas bristled.

'Just a few moments longer, sir,' said Dr Petty calmly.

'You've had your moments – now get on with the job you're here for!'

No one responded to this, but on an impulse, thinking it looked uncomfortable, Robert stepped off the bench, leaned over for Anne's dangling arm and replaced it gently on the table across her breast. It was icy cold to his touch and he shuddered at it. He *must* have been mistaken. There could not still be life within this cadaver. She was a dead thing, all animation gone and as cold as stone.

Dr Petty stared at the corpse for a long moment, puzzled, shaking his head. 'We should, perhaps, ask Dr Bathurst for his opinion.'

'Someone could go to Brasenose for him,' said Mr Clarke. But no one offered.

Suddenly Wilton gave a shout. 'God's teeth! Her eye *did* move. I just saw it!'

Sir Thomas Reade gave a cry of anger, and there was a

thud as the body of Nathaniel Frisk the surgeon slumped to the ground in a faint.

The two doctors exchanged glances. 'Was it a nervous twitch you saw,' Dr Willis asked, 'like that of a chicken when its throat's cut?'

'I've seen a headless chicken run across the common, sir!' one of the scholars said, and there was some uneasy laughter.

'Dammit, the girl was hanging in the prison yard from seven-thirty until eight of the clock!' Sir Thomas said in an explosion of rage. 'She was hanged by the neck until dead, as the law required. A doctor certified her dead.'

Robert shouted something unintelligible. It was meant to be the word *Again!* but that didn't matter, for this time everyone could see Anne's eyelids trembling, both of them; the thin, lilac-hued skin quivering as if straining to open upon the world.

There were loud cries, gasps and a general consternation in the room; Robert found that his whole body was shaking with fear and excitement. Sir Thomas gave a roar and stepped towards Anne's body, his hands raised as if he would strangle her himself. Norreys, whom Robert had heard was secretly a Catholic, fell to his knees and made the sign of the cross. 'Oh, glory!' he cried. 'She lives!'

At any other time the scholars would have been aghast

at this flagrant display of popery; now they scarcely noticed. Everyone looked to the two doctors.

Dr Willis said, 'There is the hand of God in this.'

And he and Dr Petty put down their dissection instruments.

CHAPTER ELEVEN

The morning after the announcement of Master Geoffrey's betrothal I went over to Home Farm to collect some duck eggs. I was crossing the driveway on my way back, my basket full, when I heard the sound of horses' hooves and wheels on the road outside and turned to see a pretty blue and white carriage coming through the gates with two bay horses afront, lifting their legs in an elegant trot.

I knew who must be inside the carriage and could easily have slipped around the house and gone in through one of the back doors, but was caught by an intense longing to see the person who alighted. Hesitating too long, I then had to move behind the laurel hedge and conceal myself from the arrivals.

The coach circled the drive and stopped at the front door, then the footman jumped down and lowered the steps. Master Geoffrey got out and turned to help someone else down, and I held my breath, fixed and staring as if my life depended on it. In a moment Miss Clementine de Millet appeared and I had some small comfort in seeing that she wasn't beautiful, for she had an olive skin and a long thin nose which was pushed into the air as if she detected a bad smell. She was small and delicate, however, and dressed very finely in a blue flowered dress and, over it, a yellow taffeta cloak lined in the same blue. Her dress was of a design I'd seen in Woodstock, with a ruching at the front showing an abundance of yellow petticoats, and as she lifted it slightly in order to climb down the steps I saw that she had dainty blue leather mules.

Master Geoffrey made a great show of helping her from the carriage and offering her his arm to walk to the house, as if she was a wisp of a creature who could not proceed unsupported. As they strolled across the drive I saw him point in a genteel manner to various things, such as the huge maple tree, the herd of dairy cows and the pretty aspect of the church spire between the poplar trees, and I dare say he was speaking of his family's wealth in the own-ing of such an estate. He also pointed to the dovecote and I wondered what he was saying about it. Not, I determined, that it was a place in which he'd begged and implored a housemaid to give up her chaste ways and lie with him.

The two of them hesitated a moment at the foot of the marble steps which led into the house and looked over to the farm, and I felt a moment's fear that they would take a turn around the grounds and discover me behind the hedge, but Mistress de Millet's lady-in-waiting was close behind them, and the footman with her luggage, and so they went in.

I stayed behind the hedge for some while, trying to compose myself and still the thumping of my heart. It was true, then. He really was betrothed. And it was then that I knew myself to be as stupid as a quince pudding, for in spite of what Ma and Jane had said, in spite of every sensible part of me knowing it could *not* be true, all this time I'd been secretly telling myself that Master Geoffrey might have played fair; that he loved me and in time would raise me.

I, mistress of Dun's Tew? I thought of the dainty girl I'd just seen in her elegant gown and blue leather mules, then looked down at my sturdy feet in their wooden pattens, at my stained apron, at my chapped and begrimed hands with their bitten nails. No, I would never be a mistress, no, not even of a rag shop or a brewhouse!

I became full of misery then and fell to weeping, wondering how I was going to survive. I wished myself dead and Master Geoffrey too, cursing him and praying that he would be struck down by the falling sickness and die most horribly. I could not bring myself to go into the house, for my face was red and blotched (and I knew that the rest of the servants would be sure to deduce what I'd been crying about) so left my basket outside the back door and took myself across the yard and into the dovecote. Here I climbed a stepladder into the darkness and squeezed myself onto a wooden platform to sit among the cooing birds, the droppings, the feathers and the scraps of down floating on the air. Once there, well hidden, I felt I could have stayed for ever, for to my simple way of thinking it seemed that the doves would look after me and would not deceive and trick me as Master Geoffrey had; that I could trust them more than I should ever have trusted him.

After some time, though, I stopped weeping, grew cold and began to fear what they'd be saying at the house about me, so was too frightened *not* to return. I went back very solemn, anxious about how I might be punished for my disappearance, but the house was in such a tipsy-topsy state with preparations for Master Geoffrey's betrothal supper that my disappearance had hardly been noticed. I was brought down with melancholy, however, and when I was sent to the herb patch for pungent herbs to stuff a goose that afternoon, I could not help but look across to the smithy and recall the washing day when I'd first begun speaking to John Taylor. I missed him greatly at that time, and was so unhappy that the dishonourable notion came upon me that I might bring myself into his favour again, and lie with him, and pretend that the child I carried was his own.

He was not to be seen over the road, however, and thankfully such a wicked idea was soon gone from my head. Yet I shed more tears thinking of John's kindnesses to me, and his gentleness, and how wicked I'd been to cast him off so cruelly when he had truly cared for me.

My situation seeming to have no solution, when I returned to the kitchen I didn't protest when Mrs Williams said I was to scour out all the slop buckets and chamber pots, for it seemed fitting to my mood and situation that I should be set such a horrid job – and even seeing that Susan had been set to the pretty task of making spun-sugar nests to go over candied apricots for the party did not make my disposition worse. Nothing could do that.

Everyone was eager for news of the new young lady's arrival and Patience, who was maid to Lady Mary, told us that she'd seen Mistress de Millet at dinner that noon. She reported that she was a pretty, fresh young thing and had been wearing costly jewels, although her complexion was rather brown and her nose slightly on the long side.

'She seemed very ladylike, though,' she said. 'She eats very dainty with her fork and knows just how to act. And I heard them say that she embroiders so neatly and with such fine stitches that the end result is like a painting.'

'What was she wearing?' asked Susan.

'A satin dress with an embroidered bodice and a line of ribbon knots all down the back,' Patience answered. 'And it was in a flame colour, which they said, being orange, was a play on the name of Clementine.'

All the female servants drew breath at the wit of this device which, however, did not strike me as clever at all, especially with a brown complexion.

'And does Master Geoffrey dote on her?' Mrs Williams asked.

'Oh, yes, he does!' Patience replied. 'And 'tis nice to see him so, for I've sometimes thought him a selfish young man.'

'Does he carry out little duties?' Susan wanted to know.

Patience nodded. 'He looked after her fan and shawl, and led her to the table and saw her seated, and altogether acted as if he was very much in love with her, paying her little compliments and the like.'

Jacob gave a snort of derision, which I was pleased about, but the women there gave him a cold look and said that he shouldn't be so scathing, and 'twould be a good thing if all men were more mannerly. Susan said, 'What a pretty sight they must be together!' and glanced at me as she said it.

Later that day I determined that I must appeal to Master Geoffrey and tell him of my situation, for if I was not to end up in the parish workhouse I would soon be in dire need of a place to lay my head. I wished that I had some money put by and need *not* appeal to him, but as I sent most of what I earned home to Ma, I had only a few pence to call my own. My only possessions were my clothes – I could sell my bodice, of course – and the wedding ring of my grandma, although this would not fetch much, for it was but poor gold and had worn as thin as a hair over the years.

Speaking to Master Geoffrey alone was, I knew, going to be monstrous difficult, for it was only the footmen who served dinner and the ladies' maids who were allowed about the house when visitors were within. I was, however, determined to try, for what would become of me if I did not?

The guests arrived (including, so we heard, Mistress de Millet's parents) and supper was served at seven o'clock. It had not been possible for me to get anywhere near Master Geoffrey before this, for most of the afternoon he'd been in the library deep in conversation with Sir Thomas, and someone had seen a gowned man of the law arrive bearing parchment and seals, which Mr Peakes had said was sure to be something to do with the marriage settlement. After the family and guests had eaten supper, we servants cleared away and washed the dishes, so by the time eleven o'clock came I was dropping with tiredness and also felt ill, which I thought was likely to be fear because of what I knew I must do. Susan went to bed, as did most of the other staff, so that in the end the only servants sitting up were those who waited on their master's or mistress's coming to bed. This didn't look like being for some time, however, for a group of fiddlers had come to the house and some of the company had moved from the dining room to the great hall, and were dancing.

I went to bed but crept out of the room when Susan was asleep and sat on the servants' stairs listening to the music and gaiety from downstairs. If I'd known then what was going to happen and the intentions of the Reade family towards me, then I believe I would not have sat there so patient. I believe I would have gone down those stairs into the great hall and spoken my piece in front of everyone. Oh, what a disturbance I could have caused if only I'd been brave enough! Mistress de Millet's face would have shown stunned disbelief, Master Geoffrey's would have been red and horror-struck, his grandmother would have had a shrieking fit and his grandfather would have roared with rage. What a harum-scarum cockfight I could have caused in the great hall that night!

But of course I didn't dare do any such thing, but stayed on the stairs and every now and again, when I heard a door open, ran to my bedroom and hid until I felt it was safe to go out again. I believe I fell asleep at some time, for when I woke there was no noise from downstairs and it seemed that the merrymaking had ceased. It felt safe, therefore, to go through the baize door into the family's quarters and onto the bedroom landing, and to creep along in the shadows until I came to Master Geoffrey's room, where a faint line of light under the door told me that his candle was still burning.

I pressed my ear against his door, shaking with cold and fright. I knew, of course, that Mistress de Millet wouldn't be in there, for *her* body would be held sacred until they were married, but I feared that his valet might still be in attendance. All I could hear, though, was Master Geoffrey humming, and I felt angry when I heard this, for it seemed to me to be the hum of a contented man who has everything planned and neat in his life and cares nothing about what unhappiness he might have caused along the way of it.

I tapped on the door, but so tentative was I that he didn't hear it. I tapped again, then gently pushed at the door and peered round it, ready to turn tail and run if I had to. It opened a little, and I saw Master Geoffrey at the washstand pouring himself a glass of water from a jug. He was wearing only a nightcap, had nothing on beside to hide his nakedness, and cut such a comical figure that I might have laughed at him had I been there for any other reason.

I tiptoed into the room. 'Master Geoffrey . . .' I began,

and he jumped, turned and saw me, and attempted to hide his private parts with the water jug. Why he did this I had no idea, for every other time I'd seen him he'd been only too anxious to have them on display.

'Out!' was the first word he said to me. As if I was a cur, or a cat to be chased off the soused herrings.

'Sir, I am most anxious to speak to you—'

'Out, I say!' he said in a harsh whisper. 'At once!'

'Sir, I . . .'

He looked at me with great disdain. 'Are you so hot, woman, that you have to come to my room and lay siege to me?'

I was astonished and outraged at this, but before I could give him a reply I heard the handle of the door to the adjoining room rattling, as if someone had put a hand upon it, and in my imagination saw Sir Thomas coming in, perhaps to acquaint his son with the results of some conversation he'd had with Mistress de Millet's father. I immediately reversed the two steps I'd taken in and, very shaken, backed out of the room as quickly and silently as I'd entered.

The next morning we were up at five o'clock as usual, although I could barely drag myself out of bed for weariness. My only hope of speaking to Master Geoffrey, I knew, was to catch him in his room. Accordingly, after doing my morning chores, I put a washing jug to one side and hid it in the buttery. Later, after the warm water for the family had been sent up and when Mrs Williams was occupied elsewhere, I took up the jug and carried it to Master Geoffrey's room. If anyone had seen me, they would merely have thought I was bringing him fresh water.

The curtains around his bed were open but he was still asleep, and as I looked on his sleeping form I was filled with a hatred such as the Bible says we never should feel, e'en toward our greatest enemies. Oh, I'd been stupid and I'd been lewd, but those were my only sins; Master Geoffrey's were surely much worse, for he had cruelly used and deceived me, taken advantage of his position as Sir Thomas's heir and got me with child.

With this at the forefront of my mind, I became bold enough to shake his shoulder. 'Sir,' I said. 'Master Geoffrey . . .'

He must have recognized my voice, for he immediately turned away and burrowed further into the bed.

'Master Geoffrey. I must speak with you.'

There was no reply.

I called him again, and again. Desperately, I shook him more harshly and moved the drapes around the bed to cause a draught. At last he opened his eyes.

'What is it you want?' he asked coldly, every trace of the

MARY HOOPER

sweet-talking flattery, every one of the wheedling phrases he'd used before now disappeared.

'I need to speak to you most urgently,' I said.

'How dare you come to my room!'

'I came because I am desperate, sir. I am in an impossible situation.'

'Get out now, or I'll call George and have you thrown out. 'Tis disgraceful you should beard a fellow in his room in this way.'

'But, sir, I beg you.' He closed his eyes and seemed about to go back to sleep, so I shook his shoulder again. 'Sir, I must tell you that I am in a certain condition. I . . . I am with child.'

There was a moment's silence, then, opening both eyes and seeming immediately to be fully awake, he said, 'Then 'tis not mine.'

I stared at him, stunned, for in spite of my low opinion of him, I'd never considered that he might deny he was the father, nor hardly thought that a gentleman might do such a thing. At that moment, so much did I hate him that if I'd had a knife in my hand I would have run him through with it and taken the consequences. 'But I have not lain with another man!' I said, astonished.

He did not say a word.

'I never have! You must believe me!'

But he had gone back to being a stone again, his eyes tight shut, his face set stern, his mouth a hard line. I tried again and again to garner some response from him, but could not. In the end, frightened of being discovered there, I had no recourse but to leave.

I returned to my duties, not speaking with anyone but doing as I was bid without question, my mind running frantically in all directions. Should I leave the household now, before it was discovered that I was with child, or should I stay and get a little money put by? Should I return home? Would my father, who is not known for either his patience or his tolerance, allow me to stay with them, or would he insist I went into a workhouse? What would I do when the child was born? Perhaps, I thought grimly, I would swaddle it, bring it to the house and leave it on the doorstep with Master Geoffrey's name on it.

He was to leave Dun's Tew that same afternoon, for I heard that Mistress de Millet was taking him as far as Oxford in her carriage, where he would stay one night and then catch the coach back to London. But I had obviously given him a fright with my words, for he appeared in the servants' quarters about midday saying he had a gold angel that his young lady's parents had left for the waiting staff. (I was in the dairy straining the buttermilk and became so anxious on seeing him there that I quite forgot to put salt in the butter, so that after two days it went rancid.)

After speaking to Mr Peakes and giving him the money for distribution to the servants he came to the dairy and, standing by the door in a casual attitude, said in a low voice, 'There are ways to order these things. You must get rid of the child.'

''Tis too late for that,' I said, my hands trembling as I held the muslin taut. 'And besides, I have tried.'

'Then you have not tried hard enough.'

I didn't reply.

'How do I know that you haven't got yourself with child deliberately so as to obtain money from me?'

'Begging your pardon, sir,' I said, 'but I cannot get myself with child on my own.'

'You knew what you were doing well enough! 'Twas not your first time.'

I didn't answer this, for I was too angry to control myself and felt that I might begin weeping. Either that or strike out at him.

'If you tell anyone that 'tis mine—'

'It *is* yours!' I burst out. 'As God is my witness it is your child!'

'Then I'll deny it. My family – my grandfather – will never believe you.'

I sighed aloud when he said this, for I knew he spoke truly. Sir Thomas doted on him and would be bound to take his side whatever the circumstances. 'And besides, I will get George and some of the menservants to say that they have also lain with you.'

Oh, how I loathed him then! And how it tormented me knowing that within me I carried his offspring. Struggling to keep from weeping, I scraped the butter onto the marble tile and began to form it into a block with the wooden spades. 'If you shame me like that,' I said in a low voice, 'then may you be cursed for your lies, and may God reveal you for the wicked Devil you are.'

He replied immediately, 'I will tell them that you cursed me, and you will be taken away for a witch!'

I turned on him angrily. 'If they would take me from here then they cannot come quickly enough, for I rue the day I ever came through your door!' I said, and as I spoke I formed the butter into an oblong, then gave it such a mighty bang with one of the spades that soft drops of yellow spattered up into the air and fell onto the marble. I closed my eyes for a moment in despair, and when I opened them he'd gone.

I wondered after if I should have spoken to him soft and pretended that I cared for him, for that might have been a better way. I should have used honeyed words and sweet talk, and assured him that his betrothal to Mistress de Millet would not alter things between us and I would still allow his liberties. Then, when he was won over and confident of my fidelity, I could have told him of the child and asked for his help. I did not do any of those things, however, and later spent many hours cursing my temper.

Now, though, I know that whatever I'd said to him it wouldn't have changed things.

I make one more effort to open my eyes, straining to see what's about me in the darkness, but it does me no good, for I am nowhere . . .

CHAPTER TWELVE

For a moment everything halted. The doctors and scholars who surrounded the corpse formed a tableau around Anne Green, whose body seemed rapt between Heaven and Earth. She neither lived, nor was she wholly dead.

Robert gazed at Anne unwaveringly. He knew that something strange, something problematic and meta-physical was happening. A choice was being presented to the physicians: they could decide to give her succour, or assist in her peaceful passing.

Suddenly the scene re-animated. The doctors began moving into place around the body, the scholars crowded forward. Nathaniel Frisk was pulled into a corner and left, slumped sideways, to recover on his own as best he could.

'We must help her breathe,' Dr Petty said urgently.

'I agree,' Dr Willis said. 'Shall we sit her up? Warm her?'

'*What?!*' roared Sir Thomas Reade.

'Chafe her legs, perhaps,' suggested Mr Clarke.

'*Hold!*'

A voice rang out from the back of the room and Robert

turned to see a figure in clerical black, his white collar and tall hat marking him out as a Puritan.

'Now we shall have fun,' Wilton said.

Robert looked at him enquiringly.

'Puritans cannot tolerate anything upsetting the rightful order of things,' he whispered. 'The man has wandered in to watch a dissection, and instead found a resurrection.'

The Puritan's right hand was raised, finger pointing up like that of an avenging angel. 'Hold, I say. That woman belongs to God, and God alone! You will not take her back from Him!'

Chapter Thirteen

A month later I was still at the Great House at Dun's Tew, lacing myself into my bodice and stomacher each morning and pulling them a little tighter betimes. I'd not left the Reades' household, for a lethargy seemed to have come over me so that I had neither the energy to leave, nor the courage to go home and face my father. I knew I should have told Ma of my situation, or at least got a message to her, for it was probable that she thought the cunning woman's cordial had been effective, but I did not wish to cause her any more distress. As well as this, I could not have faced the walk back to my village, for my legs ached mightily and I was constantly weary.

I could not decide how to act or what to do. Having been instructed and ordered all my life, I now longed for someone to command me in this. I felt I was waiting for something to happen – but what this thing was, I didn't know. Perhaps it was for someone to discover I was with child and help me, or for Master Geoffrey to return, own to his obligations and give me a little money to aid me, or even to summon the strength to open the door of the house, walk out and keep on walking – for I wouldn't be the first young woman to cross to a parish where she wasn't known and beg aid for herself and her unborn child. In the meantime I went about my duties and tried not to think too much about my situation. With some little effort I was able to pretend to myself that it wasn't happening.

I hardly spoke to the other servants. On the fifth of November the household celebrated Gunpowder Plot day and we were allowed to have a bonfire in the evening, but I didn't care to be present. I began to be called Mistress Nose-in-air by some and knew that they were gossiping about me, but couldn't bring myself to care. Now that I had a *great* concern in my life I marvelled at the trivial things which had occupied me before, at how much I'd fretted about an uncompleted job, a torn petticoat or a missing gewgaw, whereas now these trivialities hardly touched me and I would go for several days with a piece of lace hanging from my gown or my hair awry.

My undoing came on the first day of December, however, for this day Mrs Williams set me to work in the brewhouse stirring a great quantity of malt in a barrel. This was feverish hard work and back-breaking, and the smell of the barley was cloying and sickening to my stomach besides. I stirred and stirred with the great wooden paddle until my back felt almost broken, and only paused at dinner time when Mr Peakes sent in half a loaf and a chunk of cheese for me. After I'd eaten I began stirring again – for every so often Mrs Williams would look in on me to make sure I wasn't slacking – and it was then that I began to get the pains.

At first I was full of joy, for these were low-down pains in my belly, as if my courses were beginning anew, so I felt that my prayers might have been answered. The cramps grew more severe, however, and I went out to the far privy, which was some distance off across the yard, and there came from me a quantity of liquid which did not seem to be urine and was, I thought (for I remember being told so by Ma), that certain watery substance that women lose when they are about to give birth. I became very anxious then, for I knew I had not gone full term with the child and wondered what it meant and if I was about to bleed to death.

I sat on the privy, still and anxious, and after a bit the pains seemed to pass. I went back into the brewhouse and stood for a while leaning on the paddle, and once when Mrs Williams passed by pretended to stir the malt. After perhaps an hour the pains started again though, worse than before, and I went again to the house of office.

As the surges grew worse and came closer together, I

became terrified, for I knew that delivering a child was hazardous, and without a midwife or anyone in attendance I might die. I tried to cast my mind back to the birth of a neighbour's child that I'd attended with Ma, although I'd only been eleven years old then and could barely remember how things had been ordered. My duty had merely been to fetch warm water and sponge the woman's face and hands, and this I'd done and had never once looked below at her private parts, nor wanted to, just been glad that this was the province of the midwife. *That* neighbour had had a bed to lie on, however, and old remedies to aid her safe delivery. She'd had a piece of jasper tied to her thigh, warming broths to sustain her, linen sheets beneath her and gossips and goodwives to comfort her.

In the privy, I had none of these. And I know now that no woman should go through the perils of childbirth unaided, for it sets you in such a deal of terror that you almost lose your wits.

I undid my stomacher and removed my skirt, but after that could not think how I should conduct myself: should I stand or sit, or perhaps lie on the floor – although this was dirty and covered with blown-in leaves and other rubbish. I was afraid, though, that if I sat on the only available place, which was the privy itself, then the child might come from me and fall into the mire before I could catch it.

As the sun went down it got much colder, and I had not a shawl with me, nor a candle to see what I was doing, and I feared that someone might come into the adjoining privy and hear my moans and cries. I wondered how long my labour would be and thought of tales I'd heard from Mrs Williams, one of a woman five days in labour, and another who had been unable to give birth at all because the child had been lying across her belly instead of head down, so both mother and babe had died. I began to sob in fear, then, and wanted my ma there, and wished even for Mrs Williams or Susan to come and aid me. I thought about getting myself back to the house, but at this stage knew it would have been beyond me to walk across the cobbles; that the twenty yards might as well have been twenty miles.

In the end the pains got so bad that I picked up one of the sticks from the floor and bit it to stop myself from screaming out. And then there came a time when the pains came all the time and there was no gap between them to pause and think about what was happening, and I wanted to scream but could not even find the breath or the space to do so. My body felt it was being ripped, and I fell onto the ground and writhed about, and somehow found myself on my back with my legs against the privy door and at last, with one mighty effort, pushed the child within me out and onto the ground.

I had one short moment of blessed relief, and then I looked down at the child to see how it fared and was immediately filled with horror, for it was very small and blue in colour, with a wax-like substance over its body. Maybe I should have picked it up – and I have heard of shepherds who will breathe into a dead lamb's mouth to revive it – but in truth I was terrified of the sight of it, for it seemed such a frightening and unfamiliar thing, and not like any babe I had ever seen, nor hardly human at all. And even while I looked down at it the pains began again and I knew I had to expel the afterbirth, and this, thankfully, came out from me quickly with a gush of blood.

I lay there after, shivering and crying, and all the time I watched the child that I had given birth to and it neither moved nor breathed. It was only as long as a man's hand and its features were indefinite, although I could see it should have been born male. It looked very pitiful lying there so raw and cold and, though I couldn't bring myself to take it up and hold it, I tore a strip of linen from my petticoat and wrapped it around its body so that it wouldn't lie quite naked on the ground.

All this while I had been lying on the floor in a mess of blood, leaves and debris, my mind a blur of confusion. I couldn't think of how I was going to order things. *What was I going to do with the child?* Once I'd had a puppy dog that had died, and my pa had dug a hole and buried it in the garden. Would I have the strength to dig a hole on my own, I wondered, with the ground froze so hard? Besides, shouldn't this child have some little sanctity? It had never drawn breath, but surely it should be due more reverence than a puppy dog. Perhaps, I thought, I would hide it for now, then on the morrow, when I was feeling stronger, take it to a little spot in the churchyard and find a place to lay it down.

At this point someone came over to the privy next to mine – one of the men, for I heard him whistling – and I wondered whether to call out and ask for help, or for a woman to be sent to me. I did not, however, for I was thinking that it might be possible for me to hide all the evidence of what had happened so that it would not be discovered I'd ever been with child, and thus could go on as before.

Accordingly I sat there as still as a fallen pippin and did not make a sound, and when the fellow had gone, pushed the dead infant to the back of the privy and took up leaves and other material to cover it, for I was resolved by then to go back the next day and take its corpse into the graveyard. I'd wrap its body in a decent piece of cloth – I thought of my pretty bodice – say a prayer over it; and perhaps in the summer I'd plant a pansy or a daisy over where it lay in the ground, for they say that children like the friendly faces of these flowers. Thinking then on the poor dead babe (unwanted by anyone on Earth, which I believe was why it had died), I began to cry again but weakly, like a kitten cries, for I had hardly any strength left to do more.

When this ceased, I tidied myself as well as I could, shook out my skirt and put it back on, then resolved to go back in the house and hide myself away in my bedroom. When I came to stand up, however, I discovered that my legs were as unsteady as sea legs, and I staggered and fell down again, and had to drag myself up and lean on the wall for some moments. When I felt ready to set off I opened the privy door and took several deep breaths of frosty air before making my way across the cobbles in the darkness, shuffling my feet like some old woman.

At length I found myself at a back door of the house and, as I opened the door onto candlelight and warmth, felt immense relief at being amongst the living again; thankful that I had not perished giving birth but had come through my ordeal. I could not go and be churched as did other happy mothers, but I resolved that next Sunday I'd say a private prayer of thanks for my life, and another for the soul of the child who'd not lived.

Slow and timorous of step, I walked along the hall towards the back stairs, touching my palm against the wall every now and again to steady myself. As I did so, Susan came hurrying towards me, looking agitated.

'Why, wherever have you been?' she said. 'We've searched everywhere in the house for you!' I was surprised at this speech, which was more words than Susan had spoken to me in months. Before I had a chance to reply, however, she gave a scream. 'But what disorder you're in. What's happened? Have you had an accident?'

I should have said yes, that I'd fallen over outside or that a passing carriage had struck me in the dark, but I was not thinking properly or quickly enough.

A torch on the wall suddenly flared then, enabling her to see my appearance more clearly, and her face registered horror. 'Why, Anne Green, whatever have you done?' she asked.

'Susan,' I began tentatively, and I took a step towards her, holding out my hand in entreaty, whereupon she screamed and moved away, staring at it in horror, for there was blood on it. 'I can explain,' I said, though I had scarce thought of what I was going to say. 'Give me a moment. Let me tell you . . .'

'No!' she said, seeming genuinely fearful.

'I've done nothing wrong,' I protested.

'Mrs Williams!' she screamed at the top of her voice. 'Mrs Williams – come here quickly!'

'No,' I said. 'Please don't . . .'

But Mrs Williams hurried through within moments and, looking me up and down, seemed to take in the situation straight away. She said with a gasp, 'I *thought* you were with child. Didn't I say that, Susan? You've just given birth, haven't you?'

Susan gave a scream of horror.

'That's right, isn't it? But where's the child?' Mrs Williams asked, looking up and down the hallway as if I might have concealed it there.

I took a step, swayed and almost fell over.

'You must tell us where it is,' Mrs Williams demanded. 'You must tell us now.'

I stared at her. This was not what I'd planned.

'Everyone will find out about it. You'll not be able to keep it to yourself,' she said, and indeed I could see through to the kitchen where Mr Peakes and the other servants were, and they'd stopped going about the business of preparing supper and were looking at us with curiosity. I knew then that I wasn't going to be able to keep what had occurred a secret, for I'd not the strength to begin the construction of a story which would cover my present appearance and demeanour. Besides . . . oh, besides, I felt I'd been alone in this long enough and needed to share with someone all that I'd been through, to unburden myself to someone who'd help.

'Now, where have you left the child?' she asked again.

''Tis in the privy . . .' I answered up obediently.

'The *privy*? It's still there?' On a nod from me, Mrs Williams patted Susan on the shoulder. 'Go out there with a candle and a shawl and bring the babe inside, for 'tis a bitter cold night and e'en a bastard child deserves warmth and succour.' Addressing me, she added, 'Why, whatever were you thinking of, leaving a new-born babe outside?'

I know I should have told her the truth of it then, but could not because my body had begun to shake and my teeth to chatter violently. As Susan hurried off, Mrs Williams put her arm about me, led me into the kitchen and sat me down close to the fire, and this unusual and unexpected kindness on her part so affected me that I began to weep and could not stop.

'Now,' she said, beckoning to Mr Peakes with some urgency, 'you must tell us who the father is, and tell us truly, and we will try to help you.'

But before I could consider what I should say to this, there was a scream from outside. A terrible scream. And I knew that Susan had discovered the infant's corpse.

A moment later she came running in, crashing through the door, her hands raised, high and shaking, as if she was trying to dislodge what she'd just seen from her mind and body.

Mrs Williams stood and gaped at her.

'The babe is dead!' she shrieked. 'Dead and on the floor in the dirt!'

Mrs Williams uttered a cry of horror. Mr Peakes and the rest of the servants stopped their work and stood staring and gasping.

I was terribly affrighted and didn't know what to do next, bar continue weeping.

'You killed it, Anne Green, didn't you?' Susan said. 'You went and killed it so that no one would find out about it!'

'Oh, you wicked creature!' said Mrs Williams, and there was no kindness in her voice then, for she looked at me as if I'd crawled out of Hell and still bore the marks of the Devil on my skin.

'I did not . . . did not kill it!' I said, choking on my sobs. 'I gave birth to it out there, but it never drew breath. On my mother's life I promise that it didn't breathe.'

No one spoke, but Susan screamed again, high-pitched. 'What a sight! I never want to see the like again!'

'I didn't kill my own child!' I said, tears running down my face. 'That would be wicked – the Devil's work. No girl could do such a thing as that!'

Mr Peakes stepped forward. 'That's enough said. 'Tis the first I've heard of this but 'tis a bad business, a *terrible* business.'

'I suspected . . . I thought all along she was with child,' Mrs Williams said.

'But I didn't—' I began.

Mr Peakes stopped me. 'Before you say any more, Anne,' he said, 'Sir Thomas will have to be told of this.'

'No! Please . . .'

'Indeed he will. And it will have to be investigated properly, for a dead child is a shocking thing, whatever the cause.'

I think I lost consciousness then, for the kitchen swayed around me and I fell into a welcome blackness where I did not have to think more. The last thing I heard was Susan screaming, 'Oh, I'll never forget the sight of it as long as I live!'

When I opened my eyes, Mrs Williams was waving a singed bunch of rosemary under my nose and the smoke from it was in my eyes and mouth, making me cough.

'She's back with us now,' she said. 'Back and can answer to the wicked deed she's done.'

I coughed again, rubbing my eyes, and when I fully came to was alarmed to discover that Sir Thomas and Lady Mary had been summoned to the kitchen and were standing there in front of me. I was so disquieted by this that I felt my head swim and was like to have fainted again, except that Mr Peakes was holding a cordial to my lips and telling me to take sips of it. This drink restored me some-what, but did not lessen my terror, for I'd never seen both my master and mistress together in the kitchens before, and to know that I was the one who'd caused them to be there was most alarming.

'She's back with us, sir,' said Mr Peakes.

Sir Thomas bent down until his florid face was just inches from mine. 'What is this terrible, *shocking* tale I've heard?' he asked, while Lady Mary, who was wearing a bolero fashioned from white doves' feathers sewn onto silk, stood a little behind him. She looked, I thought, most indignant at finding herself in the domicile of her servants. 'Answer me, girl.'

'And you must tell Sir Thomas the truth, mind,' Mr Peakes said.

'Or it will surely be the worse for you,' Mrs Williams added.

I merely blinked round at them. I saw that, apart from these, all the other servants were grouped at the far end of the kitchen, watching us intently, and that work on the family's supper had stopped. The only sound was the rhythmical clanging of the wheel in the fireplace where the dog ran to turn a pig on the spit.

'You have had a *child* . . . in the house of office?'

Sir Thomas asked. 'Can this shocking thing be true?'

I didn't reply and Mrs Williams said, ''Tis true indeed, sir. Susan found the dead infant concealed under some leaves.'

Sir Thomas addressed the room. 'And did any of you here know that she was with child?'

Everyone shook their heads.

'Although I had my suspicions,' Mrs Williams said roundly, 'because she's a secretive jade. Though it's not something as you can ask a girl who's unmarried.'

'I thought she was!' Susan called over, very self-righteous. 'For she's been mighty private when she's been getting dressed of a morning.'

'Then all this should have been reported to Mr Peakes,' said Sir Thomas, 'and he would have told me, and arrangements could have been made for her admittance to a suitable establishment.' He cleared his throat. 'And the child is dead, you say?'

'I have been out and looked myself, sir,' Mrs Williams said. ''Tis stone dead right enough.'

Sir Thomas looked at me sternly. 'How did it come to die, pray? What hand did you have to play in the poor unfortunate's demise?'

I found my voice. 'Please, sir, it was dead-born,' I said. 'It didn't draw breath at all.'

Lady Mary shuddered and the dove-feather jacket shivered and trembled. 'Such a thing,' she sighed. 'Here. Here in my house.'

'Is this true?' Sir Thomas asked me. 'Did you not have a hand in its death?'

I shook my head. 'Of course not, sir. Oh, never!'

'But tell me who is the father of this child,' he went on, extending his arm around the room as he spoke. 'Who is the lewd fellow you have been fornicating with?'

I know now that if I had named someone in the village or said it was a fellow I had met with but briefly, a passing pedlar, then things might have gone better for me; Sir Thomas might have believed that the child had been born dead and dealt with the matter privately. However, a strong urge within me made me want to tell him the truth. And, as I must be honest at this time for the sake of my soul, 'twas not just for truth's sake that I spoke, but more that his grandson should be brought to answer for the part he'd played in my disgrace.

'Answer me, girl,' Sir Thomas repeated. 'Who is the coarse fellow?'

'''Twas your grandson,' I answered then, as brave as I could. ''Twas Master Geoffrey who got me with child.'

CHAPTER FOURTEEN

As one, the room turned and stared at the black-hatted figure at the back of the room. 'On whose authority do you speak, sir?' Dr Petty asked him.

'On the highest authority, sir, for I am God's deputy in this world,' replied the Puritan.

'He has many deputies,' Dr Petty said mildly, his eyes still fixed on Anne Green, alert for any further movement from her.

'And you might say that I and my colleagues are also God's deputies,' put in Dr Willis, 'for we heal, cure and restore to health as the Lord did when he was upon Earth.'

'But only God Almighty can say whether someone should live or die.'

'Exactly!' Sir Thomas shouted with immense satisfaction, applauding the Puritan. 'We must not go against God, or against the law of the land, for it has been cited that Anne Green should be hanged by the neck until dead.'

'Indeed,' said Dr Willis. 'A duty which has already been performed.'

'And once dead, she should stay dead.' As Sir Thomas addressed the doctors, his voice took on a patronizing tone. 'It has *not* been cited that she should be resurrected, or that such a thing may ever be attempted.'

'I believe that my colleagues and I are working through the Almighty,' said Dr Willis after a moment. 'If he grants us the power to cause this woman to live, then it will be His will.'

'But I say that a doctor has already certified her dead!' said Sir Thomas, and his voice was a bluster and a harrumph and a roar. 'And I say again, sir, that you must get on with what you're here for!'

The doctors took scant notice of him, but Mr Clarke, aware that Sir Thomas had far-reaching powers and might take it upon himself to close his shop if he was so minded, glanced at him nervously.

Dr Petty took up the corpse's hand again. 'Anne,' he said. 'If you can hear me, squeeze my fingers.'

Everyone in the room looked keenly at Dr Petty's face, watching for any shade of change upon it. He repeated the question once more, before shaking his head and concluding quietly, 'She does not respond.'

Robert felt his own heart fall. He wanted her to be alive. He wanted a miracle.

'She does not respond because she is not there,' said the

Puritan. He looked piously towards the ceiling and beyond it. 'She is already approaching the gates of Heaven. You must let her go through. You must not try and restrain her.'

'You see!' said Sir Thomas. 'This commendable fellow knows. This true and Godly man knows one should not attempt such a thing. The woman does not respond because she is dead! This is clear to anyone but a fool.'

The doctors remained unmoved. 'Get Ralph Bathurst!' Dr Willis said abruptly. 'Someone go for Doctor Bathurst. He should be here.'

The scholars shuffled their feet. Not one of them wanted to go to Brasenose College to find Dr Bathurst, for they knew that if they did so, they might lose their position at the table and perhaps miss seeing something momentous, something marvellous and significant. The scholar closest to the door, however, was pushed outside and told to go and find him.

Robert stared at Anne's corpse intently. What was it about her that was so different from the other dead bodies whose deaths he'd attended? He thought of these: an ancient waterman who'd drowned in the Isis, his corpse bloated and swollen; a beggar so ingrained with dirt that his skin appeared as black as the rags he wore; a porter at college; an old woman killed when her carriage had overturned. None, to his mind, had been like Anne, for somehow her corpse still seemed to contain a spark . . . a kind of faint animation. Was that because her soul was still within her, or because she was still young and had died before her rightful time? Was it, perhaps, because she was innocent of the crime she was said to have committed?

And what of that other corpse – his mother? He longed for the leisure of a moment to think again of the journey down the stairs he'd made as a child, but Anne Green's body lay before him and he knew that that time was not now.

Sir Thomas left his place and walked to the window, blowing in his hands to try and warm them. He looked briefly outside at the crowd, then seemed to check himself and edged back.

'*He*, you see,' Wilton said in a low voice, nodding towards Sir Thomas, 'made quite sure that the girl was found guilty. You know why?'

Robert shook his head, trying to make up for his lack of speech by his interest and questioning expression.

'Why? Because he recently negotiated a fine marriage for his grandson – the one who is said to have got Anne with child.'

Robert looked at Wilton, startled. 'Sh . . . sh . . . she . . . ?'

'Didn't you know she bore a child?'

Robert shook his head.

'He wanted to make certain that Anne didn't live to tell the world that his grandson was responsible,' Wilton continued. 'Sir Thomas Reade is a powerful and wealthy man. What he seeks, he obtains. His word is law.'

Robert, desperate to know, dropped his voice to no more than a whisper. He also found it easier to speak that way. 'Who . . . d . . . d . . . did . . . she . . .' he began, and then, not wanting to say the word *murder*, mimed someone being garrotted.

''Twas hardly murder!' Wilton burst out, rather louder than he had meant to. ''Twas infanticide.'

'Infanticide?' Robert's mouth formed the word as he stared at Wilton.

'Not even that! The midwife at the trial said the child was hardly formed and but nine inches long. The girl had miscarried. 'Twas nothing but a stillbirth!'

'So the *midwife* said!' put in a scholar who was standing close behind them, his face and tone declaring what he thought of the honesty of that band of women.

'There was no reason for her to lie,' said Wilton, for his mother was both a midwife and a purveyor of herbs and cures. 'Hearken to this: do you know that infanticide stands alone as the only law where the accused is guilty until proven innocent?'

The scholar shrugged, uncaring, but Robert shook his head, intrigued.

'Infanticide is a cruel law which only applies to the lower classes,' Wilton continued. 'When was one of the aristocracy last hanged for such a crime? Can you tell me that?'

Robert was about to attempt another question, but Sir Thomas resumed his place just in front of them and he thought better of it. So she was hanged for infanticide, he thought, astonished. Why, if every woman whose premature child had died was found guilty of such a crime, then the gallows would be straining under the weight of them all.

If there was any justice in the world, then this woman would live . . .

CHAPTER FIFTEEN

It was Lady Mary who fainted then, falling onto the floor in a flurry of doves' feathers. Sir Thomas struck me hard around the face so that I rocked backwards on the chair. 'You wicked girl!' he cried. 'May God forgive you for such a terrible lie!'

Some of the servants ran to help Lady Mary, and Mrs Williams put a light to the charred bunch of rosemary and waved it under her nose. When she had come to somewhat, Mr Peakes and Patience picked her up and carried her between them out of the kitchen.

No one said a word. My fellow servants, all of whom might well have suspected Master Geoffrey of being the father of the child, remained mute. (Although I own I mustn't be too hard on them, for there is precious little other work in the village if they lost their positions at the manor house.)

'You must refute those words,' Sir Thomas said, trembling with anger. 'And may God forgive you for saying such a thing about my boy.'

I didn't speak, for I was shocked and dizzy from the blow, also half distracted by what had happened to me.

Sir Thomas came towards me saying he would *make* me tell the truth, and at this point Mrs Williams stepped in and said that she wished to beg his pardon, but in her opinion quiet words might do more good than hard knocks. Sir Thomas backed off from me then, breathing hard, saying that he rued the day I ever came to work for him and he'd known e'en then from my wanton looks that I was going to cause trouble within his house.

Mr Peakes returned. 'Now, Anne,' he said with some semblance of concern – and indeed he has never been cruel to me, 'you must tell us the truth about this child and how it came to die.'

'I swear that it didn't die – for it never lived!' I looked around me, desperately seeking a kind face. 'You must believe me! I would not ever kill a new-born babe, for they are helpless, innocent things and least deserve to die of any of us.'

'Would you not even think to kill it if you wished to conceal its birth?' asked Mr Peakes.

I shook my head. 'Never, sir. On my mother's life I promise you that it never drew breath. It was an early child and should not have been born. I birthed it, and it was very small and looked blue from the start.'

'Ask her again who is the father,' Sir Thomas said brusquely. 'And tell her that she must speak the truth this time or suffer the consequences.'

Mr Peakes spoke and asked the question, but I didn't answer. Knowing that my reward for the truth would be another blow, I was not brave enough for that.

'You must tell us, Anne,' Mr Peakes asked again. 'It will be best for you in the end.'

'But I *have* told you the truth.' I shot a look at Sir Thomas and felt my mouth dry up with fear and my voice catch in my throat so that I stammered. 'B . . . b . . . but I dare not say it again.'

'If you will not speak here,' Sir Thomas said, 'then you must answer for your actions in court.'

In court. I didn't really know what these words meant, what they might conceal, so he might as well have said that I should answer for my actions in a field or in the market-place. Some of the servants, though, gave a gasp, and must have realized the seriousness of my situation.

'And there in court you shall answer truthfully and before God!'

There was another long silence before Mrs Williams said in a troubled voice, 'Shall she be taken there tonight, sir?'

'No, but at first light in the morning,' Sir Thomas said.

'And she must be locked in the ice house overnight so that she doesn't escape.'

'Locked in all night?' I asked, my voice shaking, for 'tis cold as charity in the ice house, and besides, I've always been afeared of the darkness and knew that there were no windows there – no, not even a crack where the moon might shine through.

'And in the ice house, sir?' Mr Peakes added after a moment.

Sir Thomas nodded. 'For she cannot be trusted. None of you are safe in your beds whilst she is close by.'

Everyone continued staring at me, and I began to be very frightened. 'But what will happen to me?'

'Tomorrow you will go to Oxford, to the prison,' Sir Thomas said with no little pleasure in his voice, 'and in time you'll stand trial at the assize court for your crime.'

'W . . . w . . . what crime?'

'Are you dull of wit as well as wicked? For the crime of murder.'

'But I never did murder!'

'That will be for the judge and jury to decide. And if you should dare to say again that your foul fornication was with the innocent boy who is the heir of this house, then I shall add slander to that charge.'

I began weeping, as did some of the other female

servants. Mr Peakes coughed and said in a low voice, 'And what should we do with the dead child, sir?'

'It will be needed as evidence,' Sir Thomas said. 'I charge you with the task of taking a cloth and wrapping it ready to travel to Oxford with this . . . this murderess here.' He got out his pocket watch. 'I shall send horse to the prison governor tonight and ask that the cart be here at first light. In the meantime you must see that she doesn't escape.'

'Sir,' Mr Peakes said, bowing a little, 'the ice house is very cold. She may perish out there.'

'It would be as well if she did,' came the reply. 'Rather that a body should freeze to death than stand and answer to the foul charge of murder.'

'She . . . she may maliciously spoil the meat stuffs there,' Mr Peakes said with a ghost of a glance at me not to speak. 'I think, sir, if you will allow it . . . the cellars here may suffice. I shall see to it that she doesn't escape.'

'Very well,' Sir Thomas said dismissively. 'I leave it to you, Peakes.'

He went out and I curled myself up on the chair, my arms tight around my legs. I continued weeping and would not look at anyone even when they spoke to me, for I felt ill and wretched and bitterly ashamed of everything that had happened. Susan didn't venture near, but Jacob and some of the women came close by and tried to say some comforting things, although none were able to give me any solace. After a while I was given soup and a bowl of hot potatoes, and after eating these I was led down into the cellars. I was terrified at the thought of being left in darkness, but a moment after Mr Peakes locked the door it was opened again and someone – I didn't see who – put in my warm cloak, also an undersmock and some clean petticoats, which I was pleased to change into. They also left a lit candle.

After I'd dressed myself I sat on the floor and rocked backwards and forwards in an effort to warm and comfort myself. It was fearsome cold (although not as cold as it would have been in the ice house) and I was not able to sleep, being too scared of the shapes and shadows, the faint noises from around the house and the skittering and scattering of the rats to close my eyes. More than this, I had an ache in my belly and my heart and could not stop weeping, for I was in a deal of fright thinking of the morning and what it might bring, and how I could let my dear family know what had happened to me.

Very early the next morning Mr Peakes unlocked the cellar door and Susan came in with a bowl of hot oatmeal pottage and a glass of small beer on a tray. She didn't speak and looked away from me, embarrassed, when she put it down, but I saw that the pottage had some plump raisins in it and the thought came to me that she must have added these herself. I wanted to speak with her then, tell her everything that had happened and explain how I'd come to such a fall, but of course it was much too late for me to try to make a friend of her. I pressed her hand by way of saying thank you, but could do no more.

'Now, Anne,' Mr Peakes said when she had hurried away, 'you must eat up quickly and make yourself ready for the cart that will take you to Oxford.'

I began trembling. 'Am I really to go to court then, and to gaol, as Sir Thomas said?' I asked, for I had been comforting myself with the idea that this might have been an empty threat, something said in the heat of a moment – for my father has such a temper – which might be forgotten about in the morning.

'I fear that you are, Anne.'

'And what will happen to me?'

'You will go before the court and be tried, and they will decide whether or not you are guilty of killing your child.'

'But you have my word that I am not!' I said straight off.

'Then that's what you must tell the jury.'

'But what if they decide that I *have* done such a thing?'

'Then . . . then you will have to answer for it. They will'

– but he did not speak of the worst thing that could happen, although he must have known it all along – 'they will perhaps brand you on the arm. Or put you in the stocks for a time. You must prepare yourself to be brave.'

I did not speak for a while, for I was fair famished and intent on eating every bit of the pottage.

'Sir Thomas is fearful angry,' Mr Peakes said when I'd finished.

I nodded. 'But 'tis mostly because I said Master Geoffrey was the father of the child, is it not?'

Mr Peakes cleared his throat, seeming to be un-comfortable. 'If . . . you . . .' he began slowly. 'If you were to name another man as the father of the child, then matters might improve. But if you persist with saying that the infant is of Master Geoffrey's begetting, then things could go very bad. Sir Thomas is what's known as a Justice of the Peace, which is a high office of the law.'

'Name another man as the father?' I asked. 'But you've told me that I must speak the truth!'

He didn't reply for some time, then said, 'Think on this and know what's on Sir Thomas's mind, for if the family of Mistress de Millet get to hear of your accusation, then the marriage that has been negotiated between her and Master Geoffrey will be annulled and the Reade family disgraced.

The liaison between two great families will fall asunder. Do you want that on your conscience?'

'Then what are you saying?' I asked in disbelief. 'That I should lie?'

'Well,' he said slowly, 'what if, instead, you told the court that you didn't know who was the father of the child. That you had lain with half a dozen men and couldn't tell who was responsible.'

'I could not!' I said, horrified. ''Tis not true and I would not bring such shame on myself or my family.'

'Then name one other only. Name your erstwhile suitor: John Taylor the blacksmith.'

'I could not do that, either!'

Mr Peakes looked at me gravely, 'Just think on't, Anne: if you named John Taylor as the father, then Sir Thomas might relent and deal with the matter himself. You might not need to go to court.'

'But it isn't true!' How could I name John! Why, he and I had only ever held hands. Besides . . . besides, I loved him, and would not besmirch his life to save mine.

'Name him and 'twill not be so bad,' Mr Peakes went on, 'for all that will happen is that he'll be hauled before the magistrates and be made to marry you. And Sir Thomas will drop the charge of murder.'

'No!' I said. 'And anyway, John Taylor wouldn't ever

marry me, for he hates me now.' And with this I fell to weeping again and wouldn't be comforted.

A little bit later, while it was still dark, Mrs Williams came down and said that the cart and two of the sheriff's men were here from the prison to take me away. She'd done up all my possessions: some undersmocks, a tabby skirt, three jackets, my Sunday gown and a day dress. There was also the precious, hateful, silver-threaded bodice, which they must have found under my mattress. 'I have given you some foodstuffs,' she said, 'and Susan has found a comb and mirror of yours, and a gold ring and some ribbons, and we have put them all in a pocket here.' She rolled everything into a tidy bundle, which she tucked under my arm and bade me take care of, then she took my hand and, squeezing it hard, wished me God speed.

I thanked her, and thought of that which had kept me awake and crying all last night. 'How will I let my ma know?' I asked. 'How will my family learn what's happened?'

'You may rest easy on that,' Mrs Williams said, 'for Susan is to go to your cottage in Steeple Barton straight after she's finished her morning duties. And she'll relate to them all that's occurred.'

'And tell them I didn't do it!' I cried, and Mrs Williams nodded and turned away, for she didn't seem able to look me in the eye. I didn't feel that I hated her or Susan then, however, for it seemed to me that they both regretted what they'd put in motion by taking the matter to Sir Thomas.

A shout came that I was to get outside and look sharpish about it, and I stood, all of a shake, and Mr Peakes offered me his arm to help me up the stairs. Together we walked through the kitchens while the rest of the servants paused in their morning duties to wish me luck, and some of the women (perhaps having more foresight than I about what was going to happen) fell to weeping, and I found myself stopping and saying silly and comforting things to them, such as I was all right, and would be sure to be back with them before too long. And it reminded me of when Lily Grove the scullery maid had got married to a carrier two years before, and Mr Peakes had led her through the kitchens and everyone had pressed flowers into her hands and given her little trinkets for luck (although these had not worked, for she had died giving birth to her first child).

At the back door two men were waiting, and at first they looked at me very stern and spoke gruffly when they asked my name, but afterwards seemed to relent when they saw that I wasn't going to offer them any violence or resistance. I climbed into the back of the cart with some help from Mr Peakes, and sat on the floor of it with my bundle, and one of the drivers climbed in after and clasped my legs together with an iron manacle and some chains, the way I've seen highwaymen and the like pictured in the news sheets. Once secured, I crawled into a corner of the cart huddled into my cloak, and prayed that the journey to Oxford would be quick. I was pitifully ignorant of the ways of the law at that time, for I thought that the matter might be settled that afternoon; that the jury would be there waiting and, when they realized that I was not a murderess, release me. I looked in fear for Sir Thomas or Lady Mary to come out, but they did not, and I cannot say that I was glad about anything on that morning, but I was glad about this.

Mr Peakes gave me some money wrapped in a paper that he said was my wages, and we were just about to set off when he shouted to the drivers to wait a while for he'd just remembered something, and, going back to the house, came out again with a small bundle wrapped in a rough linen dish clout. I thought this must contain something that I'd forgotten and held up my hands to receive it, but Mr Peakes shook his head at me and handed the bundle to the driver, who placed it under his seat. I realized then that it was the dead infant, and was struck with mortification and pity.

It was scarce light by the time the cart trundled out of the gates of the manor house, but there were already people in the lane outside going about their morning duties.

Seeing them, I shrank back and hung my head so that my hood covered my face, for I feared they might realize that it was a prison cart and follow the usual custom of shouting after it, or of throwing old vegetables and other rubbish at whoever was being borne away. I least wanted to draw attention to myself right *there*.

To my horror, however, as the cart turned at the corner of Cow Lane to go towards Oxford, John Taylor came by on his way to work and hailed the driver of the cart to ask who was aboard, saying it was news to him that there were knaves and thieves about these parts.

I prayed with all my heart that the driver might urge the horse on without replying or John might not wait upon his words, but God was not listening, for the driver paused to adjust his cape about him and John stood his ground.

'No thieves, but one murderess,' came the reply.

'A murderess!' John asked, astonished. 'Someone from this village?'

'Aye,' came the reply.

With my eyes tight shut I heard him walk two steps closer to the back of the cart to see if he could discern who was there. All he would have seen of me, however, was a huddled black shape. 'A *murderess?*' he repeated. 'From where does she come?'

'From the manor house.' The carter whipped up the

horse and I heard John Taylor ask, 'And by what name goes this murderess?'

But just then the horse began moving and the wheels of the cart turned on the gravel and I don't know if John Taylor heard the reply that came, or even if one was uttered. I pictured him standing in the lane looking perplexed, his hands on his hips, and I ached to look at him and see his dear face once more. I did not do this, however, for I was too ashamed and, besides, feared to see the repugnance and disgust that would be writ on his features when he found out it was me.

There followed a miserable journey, for I was jogged and jostled about on the floor of the cart, and became bruised and sore, and it was so fiercesome cold that even with my cloak tight about me I shivered and shook. We went over a crossroads where a highwayman (so I heard my drivers say) hung on a gibbet, and I could not resist looking at the sight, which was terrible indeed, for the flesh of the person was near all gone so that it was a mere man of bone who hung there in an iron cage, with a bird of prey perched on his skull. We went through the villages of Gylmpton and Wootton without anyone hardly noticing the cart, but at Woodstock we stopped so that the men could take refreshment at The Feathers, leaving me chained to a stave in the back. I curled up very small again then, and remained still, so that anyone seeing me would have thought I was just a bundle of rags. Some children passed, and I heard them talking of whether there was a person in the cart, and one of them jumped in the back and kicked me. I still didn't stir, however, for I knew it would be the worse for me if I was discovered.

When the two drivers came back they were merry from the ale, and, laughing as they whipped up the horse, thought they would have some sport by shouting to passers-by what it was they carried to Oxford City. They thus began calling, in the manner of tradesmen shouting their wares, 'What ho – a murderess!' and 'Look sharp for a murderess!' and at Yarnton a group of villagers heard them and, gathering together, began to run after the cart, shouting that I should be hanged forthwith, so that I became frightened that they would pluck me out right then and hang me from the nearest tree. They beat on the back of the cart with branches, and clanged pots and pans and threw stones, and one came right up and gave me a hard poke with a sharpened stick through the bars of the cart. This tore right through my clothes and lacerated my arm, but I still did not move or utter a sound.

The journey to Oxford was perhaps twenty miles. We covered this in five hours, and it was terrible and wearisome all the way, and muddy, too, for the wheels of the cart went into potholes and puddles and splashed up water so that I was fair soaked with mud by the time we neared Oxford. I did not weep, however, for I felt that I had wept so much in the past day and night that I could weep no more, but just sat as still as a stone, infinitely weary and sick to my soul, trying to brace myself for whatever should come next.

As we entered the city of Oxford and the horse began to labour up a hill, the drivers shouted back to me that I should stir myself, for the end of the journey was in sight. At this point I peeped out from under the hood of my cloak and saw that at the top of the hill was a hideous and forbidding old castle, and knew that here lay my destiny.

Chapter Sixteen

'What next?' Dr Petty asked his colleagues with some urgency to his voice. 'What ought we to do?'

'Should we do anything?' Dr Willis replied. 'We will not dissect her at present, of course. Perhaps we should just . . . leave her.'

'Let nature take its course?' asked Mr Clarke.

'Exactly.'

No! Robert wanted to shout. Don't leave it to the healing power of nature, in case nature chooses *not* to heal.

Dr Petty put his hand to Anne's cheek where the rope had rubbed and caused abrasions to her skin. 'But . . . don't you agree that we may intervene a little?' he asked. 'Assist nature?'

'I wonder if that would be ethical,' Dr Willis answered, sounding concerned. 'Isn't the Puritan correct? Wouldn't anything we do be deemed as interfering with the will of God?'

Dr Petty shrugged. 'But God – or whoever,' he couldn't resist adding, for it was known that was a doubter, 'has chosen to leave signs of life within this woman, so surely it would be going against His wishes if we *didn't* aid her?'

'Excuse me, sirs,' one of the scholars said, 'but on the gibbet she asked that God in his wisdom should prove her innocence to the world.'

'Indeed she did,' said Dr Willis, his face clearing. 'And mayhap this is God's way of answering such a request.'

'And we are but His assistants,' said Dr Petty. He spoke with a slight mocking tone to his voice but Dr Willis didn't seem to notice.

'Is *rigor mortis* set in?' Mr Clarke asked after a moment.

Dr Petty felt along Anne's arms. 'Difficult to tell whether it's *rigor mortis* or she's frozen solid. It's so damned cold in here.' He gestured to the back row of the scholars, where the one who had sung and danced earlier stood. 'You. Kindly go and fetch more coals.'

The scholar went out, reluctantly, and Wren turned to his block of paper and began drawing a picture of Anne's recumbent body. Robert, suddenly feeling an immense frustration at the uncertainty, the indecision, the *slowness* of what was occurring, stepped forward. He didn't think of the unreliability of his speech, merely of a desperate desire to move things on; to take away that blasphemous and odious noose; that dread reminder of death.

'T . . . t . . . t . . . take r . . . r . . . rr . . . ?' he suggested.

He tried again with the r, then gave up and made gestures with his hands to show what he meant.

Dr Petty nodded. 'There would be no harm in that.'

'And then we will see what Bathurst has to say,' said Dr Willis.

Robert stepped forward, his hands shaking slightly. He lifted Anne's head, felt the cold roundness of her skull, the hard roundels of her spinal cord, the matted dampness of her hair. His fingers caught at a knot and, as he gently lifted her head from the table and felt the slackened muscles beneath the skin at the nape of her neck, he saw that she'd tied back her dark hair with a red ribband. This was damp and bedraggled, but the sight of it touched him, for he could not help but picture her in her prison cell early that morning, preparing herself for death and tying her hair back in one last feminine and practical gesture. The pity of it. The very pity of her death – especially if she had been innocent.

But perhaps she was not going to suffer death. Suddenly he was overcome with some emotion that he barely understood, and his vision blurred. Blinking hard, he manoeuvred the heavy noose over Anne's chin and up over her face, then dropped it. It landed on the floor, scattering sawdust in all directions.

Sir Thomas sighed a loud and exasperated sigh. 'I have

never before witnessed such a farrago. I'm going straight to the prison governor.'

Dr Petty leaned over and laid a gentle and restraining hand on his arm. 'Just allow us a few more moments, sir. We must make completely sure that this young woman—'

'I've already allowed you a few damn moments!' Sir Thomas pulled out a pocket watch somewhat golder and grander than Dr Petty's. 'I've been here near on fifty minutes and not a thing has been done – you haven't even started the cutting. I'm going to the prison governor now to discover the ruling on these things. If necessary, I'll have this jade hauled back to the prison yard and re-hanged.'

'And I shall come with you, sir!' called the Puritan at the back of the room. ''Tis going against the law of the land that these men should mess with corpses. She cannot be dead one moment and alive the next!'

As the two of them went together from the room, the atmosphere grew tense. Frisk, who had hauled himself to his feet, was leaning on the wall looking pale, and the only sound in the room came from Norreys, who, although not now on his knees, was muttering what sounded suspiciously like a Roman Catholic prayer. Robert hoped, for his sake, that there were no fervent anti-papists present.

The singing scholar came back with a scuttle containing hot coals and threw these onto the fire, which flared up immediately. A moment after, Dr Ralph Bathurst hurried in with snowflakes dotting his cloak and his arms full of glass jars. A slender, clever man who wrote verse in French and Latin, he had personally been hit hard by the Civil War, for six of his twelve brothers had been killed fighting for the Royalists. Calm and sociable, he tried to retain an equable disposition at all times, and, together with Drs Petty and Willis, was an enthusiastic member of the small group of natural scientists who met regularly in Oxford.

'I was on my way here and was nearly bowled over at the door by Sir Thomas Reade hurrying from the building!' He looked around the room at the rapt faces. 'But whatever's going on?'

He was told by a chorus of voices and fell to marvelling, then placed the jars along the windowsill in a row. 'I was bringing these jars to receive the woman's vital organs for preservation,' he said, 'but possibly they won't be needed.' He nodded outside. 'There's a mob down there waiting to claim her body. If they hear of this, I fear they'll break the doors down.'

'Then we must *not* let them hear of it until the matter is decided one way or the other,' said Dr Willis.

Dr Bathurst looked down at Anne, touched her cheek, bent over to check if he could hear breathing. 'But the whole story is almost unbelievable. Several of you saw it, you say?'

'*All* of us saw her eyelid move,' said Dr Petty.

'It has moved twice!' Wilton interjected, and Robert looked at him gratefully. 'And before that she seemed to croak in the back of her throat.'

'There may be nothing in it,' Dr Bathurst said. 'It may be certain fluids and humours moving about her body – but, if you both agree, I think we must give her a chance.'

Both doctors nodded and Dr Petty glanced at the scholars. 'I'm inclined to the view that we should treat this as a lesson,' he said. 'It may be disappointing to some that there's no body to dissect, but scholars may take instruction just the same.'

'Indeed,' said Dr Bathurst. 'So perhaps we should first ascertain which of her humours might be wrongly balanced.' He glanced at the students standing before him. 'What are the vital forces in the body, young sirs? And which of these four may be out of kilter in this young woman?'

But no one was willing to venture an opinion on which element might be lacking, or in excess, in the body before them.

After several moments' silence Dr Petty asked, 'So what should we do to help to restore her to the world?' He spread his hands. 'And this question is also for me and my fellow doctors, for to my knowledge such a thing has never happened before.'

Indecision clouded the room.

'Cut pigeons in half and apply them to her feet?' Norreys suggested, but this being a method regarded as rather old-fashioned, all three doctors shook their heads.

A powdered burned swallow and the dripping from a roast swan evoked similar responses.

'A cordial, perhaps?' said Dr Willis. 'Surely a restorative cordial could do no harm.'

'A cordial might be in order . . . perhaps cinnamon and sorrel mixed with rainwater?' Dr Petty bent down so that his face was very close to Anne's own, and placed his fingers on her lips, which he then pushed open to reveal small white teeth. 'Although her teeth are so hard clenched,' he went on, 'that 'twill be difficult to pour any such liquid into her mouth.'

Dr Willis lifted her right arm, held it up a moment then replaced it. 'Can you move your hand, Anne?' he asked the still form.

Robert held his breath, but nothing about her stirred.

'What should we do?' Dr Petty asked. He pounded his hand into his fist. 'We must do *something*!'

'Take blood?' Dr Willis suggested.

'Of course!' said Dr Bathurst, and the medical men nodded as one, for blood-letting was generally regarded as mandatory in all cases where a prognosis was in doubt.

Robert, hearing a movement in the corridor outside, looked towards the door anxiously, for he feared that at any moment Sir Thomas was going to return with the hangman close behind him. It was merely the lighter step of Martha, however, who was coming in with a glass of ale to help revive Nathaniel Frisk.

'I'd like someone to take notes for us,' Dr Petty said, and on Robert quickly raising his hand went on, 'for until we are certain that Anne Green is entirely dead, we must treat her as a normal patient. Someone, perhaps, who's recovering from the ministrations of some blundering surgeon.' His eye caught that of Nathaniel Frisk and he checked himself. 'I do beg your pardon, sir.'

'No offence taken, sir,' said Frisk weakly.

'We must treat her as a recovering patient,' Dr Petty went on. 'One who needs constant monitoring and care.'

Robert nodded and took out his notepad. 'I . . . I . . . I . . .' he began, and then gave up and merely held the notebook and a sharpened pencil aloft and gave a confirming nod.

Dr Petty consulted his watch, then handed it to Robert. 'The time is now eleven fifteen,' he said. 'Start with that.'

Chapter Seventeen

This soft and enclosing blackness where I can feel neither heat nor chill, hunger nor thirst, is indeed preferable to the circumstances in life in which I next found myself, which was the gaol at Oxford Castle, for there I was thrown into a big dark space more like a pit than a room. It was circular in shape, with high-up windows which had bars across them but no glass, so that the wind constantly swirled around and in and out and made a ghostly moaning sound which frightened me at night and stopped me from sleeping.

Not that I *could* sleep easily, for I found no comfort there: not a mattress, a plank, nor even straw to lie on, for most of the inmates slept either directly on the foul floor or on the stone seating ledge which ran around the outer limits of the room. This hard ledge was cold and in-hospitable, but, if you could but secure yourself a place on it, was preferable to the floor, which was damp with slime and gritty underfoot.

But I am jumping ahead of myself, for on being

rough-handled into the gaol the first thing to assault my senses had been the fetid smell. At home with Ma I'd lived constantly with the hot stink of livestock, but the stench in the gaol was much worse than this and made me retch, for 'twas a fusion of smells which – I know now – consisted of human excrement, rotting limbs, untreated sores and the foul miasma of squalor, degradation and despair. It held the stench of death, too, for three days after I'd been admitted, a crone who'd been hunched into a far corner wearing heavy leg irons was found to be dead – and to have been dead for some days, too, for when they went to move her it was discovered that her legs had quite rotted away from her body.

When, that first day, I became a little more used to this stink and was able to stop retching, I dragged myself (for I was still wearing manacles) to a space on a ledge and looked around me. What I saw was like a scene from Hell – only that Hell is hot and this was wintry cold – for some forty souls were crammed into this room, either sitting around with their faces full of despair, or walking about raving and railing against whatever had caused them to be held here. Some inmates seemed utterly mad, for there was a woman who spoke high-pitched and sobbing in a child's voice, another who did nothing but gibber like a strange animal and run up and down in the channel where we relieved ourselves, and a man who spent most of the day standing on his head against the wall.

I was terrified, of course, for I had hardly known that such a thing as a gaol existed before, nor at all what it would be like, but never could have imagined it would be as foul and offensive as this. I sat in a dark corner for some time, clutching my bundle of clothes to me without moving or drawing attention to myself, for I thought it best to observe the inmates going about and see how things were done and if there was a certain way to behave.

I quickly realized, however, that there was no pattern to the day and no set of rules to follow, for all was just confusion and beastliness. People shuffled about dragging their manacles behind them or sat, heads drooping, seemingly owned by misery. A continual wailing filled the air, and occasionally there would be a scuffle and one man would half-heartedly wrestle another to the ground, but generally they seemed too cold, ill and disheartened to bother with anything, as if the very effort of keeping themselves alive in such a place was trial enough.

It was bitter cold, and though there was a brazier in the centre of the room wherein burned a few sticks, it was surrounded by so many trying to glean its meagre warmth that it could not easily be seen, and I did not even discover its existence on that first day. There was no outside space to use, and it became apparent that everyone was incarcerated continually, with no respite from the foulness which surrounded them, and never a breath of good fresh air. The only space where the outside world could be seen was through the high windows, which afforded tiny, oblong views of sludge-grey sky way over our heads, and a barred grill in one of the walls, which opened onto a pathway through the castle, enabling prison inmates to beg alms from visitors as they walked through the grounds. When anyone passed, a beseeching and a crying would come from every nearby prisoner. 'Sire, spare a little food!'; 'I beg you madam, I am dying!'; 'I have three children and a babe to feed!' they would variously plead (for there were, indeed, several poor children placed amongst us).

I found that a small amount of old straw had been placed here and there along the concrete ledge, but when, that first night, I went to take some to sleep on, I soon discovered that each paltry clump had been bought and paid for by a prisoner, who would as soon stab you through the heart as have you take it from him.

Some time after the sun went down, perhaps about five o'clock, just as I was fearing that we were going to be left in the dark all night, a few torches were lit and put to the wall, and then one of the turnkeys came round with a great basket of dark bread and began to throw it to us, making a joke that we were all performing dogs and must catch it. Indeed, everyone saw to it that they *did* catch it because to miss would have meant it falling onto the floor, which was coated with filth, dung beetles and dead lice.

I jumped for a roll when he threw one my way, for I was very hungry, and this amused the turnkey no end and he began to roar with laughter, saying it was quite a thing to see a murderess jumping for her bread – but he thought I must have done many a good jump in my time. I hardly knew what he meant, but the jeering and hooting that came from some of the men told me that he'd been making a lewd joke. Some of them looked at me strangely after this, and I knew that they were wondering who I'd killed and if it was perhaps my sweetheart. I did not speak to them, however, or ever tell the truth but to one person, for I thought it better that they should think I was a murderess, for then they might be a-feared of me and leave me alone.

The bread was dark and solid, but I began to gnaw at it, and then remembered that Mrs Williams had given me some food. I opened this paper and found some slices of ham, a decent-sized piece of cheese, a green marchpane cake and an apple. I stared at the apple, and then I clutched it to me and began to weep, for it was a little red apple from the tree at the very front of the orchard which over-looks the lane and – it being an early fruiter – I had probably picked it with my own hands that summer, sitting in the tree's branches and calling over the fence to John Taylor at the forge. I'd been happy then, but had not realized it. Oh, how I yearned for that time again so I could order my life differently!

But through my tears I could smell the delicious aroma of the cheese, so dried my eyes on a corner of my skirt and, when I looked up, was surprised to see that I was surrounded by six or seven men and women, all staring at my food hungrily.

'Do you not want that, mistress?' one asked.

'Can you spare a little food?'

'It is several months since I had a bit o' meat.'

'I'm fair starved, so I am . . .'

I was torn by pity for them and greed for myself, for I knew that if all that was to be provided was black bread, I'd soon be in dire need of more nourishment. However, as I hesitated, each put a hand out to me and looked at me with such pleading eyes that I could do no less than place a small amount of food into each one.

Of course, as soon as the rest of the room saw what was going on, they flocked around me like the doves when I threw grain, and I had to tuck the apple up my sleeve and quickly stuff the rest of the food in my mouth or would have found myself with none at all. And so, barring the apple, by the end of that first day my food was all gone.

I didn't sleep a bit that night, for I couldn't secure a place on the ledge and had to sleep on the floor, and there was never a moment when someone wasn't wailing, screaming, pleading to be let out of the prison or begging for rope to hang themselves and be done with the place. As well as this there came horrid little noises as the rats pattered along the floor or the occasional splash as they entered the open sewer and began to eat whatever they found there. I was terrified that, if I closed my eyes, one might creep up and begin to gnaw at my finger or toe.

I spent most of that night thinking on the scrap of babe that I'd birthed and found it hard to rid myself of the image in my head of it rolled, tiny and stiff, in its linen shroud. I also wondered with horror if I might have unthinkingly killed it by neglecting it. If I'd picked it up and rocked it, or cleared its mouth, might it have lived? I could not envisage myself doing either of those things, however, for whenever I thought of handling it, it made me near shudder with dread. I couldn't think that I ever would have loved such a little creature, although I pitied it with all my heart.

The following morning there was more black bread to eat, and some gruel, which was thin and foul, and at this time I was approached by a prisoner I did not think I'd seen the previous day. She was a woman I judged to be of around thirty years of age, not too shabby in her dress and wearing a passably clean white apron and cap. Her hair was coloured red and frowsy and she had some flea bites on her face but she was not unattractive, having large and very dark eyes. She asked if I'd brought any food from home and, if so, if I had a scrap to spare.

I shook my head. 'I'm sorry but I have not, for it all went last night,' I said – although I still had my red apple up my sleeve.

'No matter,' she said, sitting down beside me, 'but how did you like your first night in the gaol?'

'I did not like it one bit,' I said and, feeling my bottom lip begin to tremble, knew that I was about to weep again. 'How do you bear to stay here? I can't see how I'll survive in such a place.'

' 'Tis not too bad for me,' she said, 'for I gets myself out of this animal den at night.'

'You go home?' I asked, looking at her in astonishment.

'No, dear,' she said. 'But I go to a gentleman's cell of an evening, and there I sleeps the night on a good feather mattress.'

I forgot my tears. 'How do you do that?'

'I'm a nightwalker, dear,' she answered. I must have looked at her uncomprehendingly for she added, 'A trugmoldy. A whore.'

'Oh,' I said, much shocked, for I had not met any woman of her occupation before, and she sounded so very bold about it.

'They picked me plying my trade under Magdalen Bridge, so while I waits to be sentenced, I does a little work here and there to keep my hand in.'

'But where are the gentleman's cells?' I said, looking around.

'They're on the floor above,' she said, and went on confidentially, 'There are all sorts there: famous and rich highwaymen, and gents who turn tricks with playing cards, and also a couple of merchants who are accused of stealing from each other. And all are very willing to pay for a lady's company of a night.'

'They have their own cells?'

'They do indeed! And some of these are nicer than my own lodgings at home, for they has pictures and hangings brought in, and food sent from the tavern, and one of the highwaymen even has his own four-poster bed. You may obtain anything here if you has the money to pay for it.' She looked at me questioningly. 'But you don't seem the regular sort of prisoner and I sees you aren't of my persuasion, so why are you here in Oxford's finest?'

I sighed and, there being precious little else to do, began to recount the story of Master Geoffrey and my downfall. And I finished by telling her, *swearing* to her, that the child was stillborn and never drew breath. 'But for all that they still say that I'm a murderess!'

She took my hand and squeezed it. 'Never fear, my dear, the truth will come out at the trial, for when you has a chance to speak you must say exactly what happened. And when the judge and jury realize that you're a truthful and honest girl, then they're sure to release you straight away.'

'But when do you think that will be?'

'Well, the judge travels about the country, but I've been told that he'll arrive here before Christmas. About the thirteenth of December, so they say.'

'How far off is that?'

We worked out that it was nearly two weeks hence, which realization filled me with acute misery. To think I had two weeks incarcerated here before I could come before the judge, tell him I'd done nothing wrong and be released. For I didn't even consider that my liberation might not happen.

'If you wish, I can find you a nice gentleman protector,' my new friend – whose name was Rebecca – said, 'and then at least you'd sleep comfortable well at night.' She gave a knowing little smile and added, 'Or you would sleep well after you'd done the business with him!'

'I could not,' I said, shaking my head. 'I was persuaded

to sleep with Master Geoffrey and it has led to my ruin. I'll never lie with another man until I'm wed. I'm certain of that.'

She looked at me consideringly. 'After you've been here a few days, you may reconsider.'

'I shall not!' I said, then added more gently (for I had a mind to keep Rebecca as a friend, whatever her occupation might be), 'But thank you for asking me.'

I found that she'd come to Oxford some eight years before, when the king had brought his court from London for safety before the war. 'I was but fifteen then,' she said. 'I was a beauty,' she went on, 'with long black hair which I wore in ringlets right down my back, and my eyes very dark and lustrous – as brown as yours are blue. My eyes! Oh, men wrote verse about them, saying they bade them come to bed.' She sighed. 'I had several admirers among the young men of the court, and they paid for my lodging and bought me dresses and pearls. Once I even had a pretty pink carriage drawn by a white horse.'

'And what happened?'

'Then the war came to Oxford and all the men went into battle, the king was captured and the city went over to parliament. But even at the start there was not so much rollicking fun to be had here as in London in the early days.'

'Was there truly not?' I asked, for I had heard as much from the ballads.

'And now 'tis all different, for everything is run by Puritans and they're all for stopping everyone's fun.'

'And have you been a nightwalker all that time?' I asked.

She nodded. 'But only for gent'men,' she said. 'I wouldn't take a farmer or a labouring man. I have some clerical gents, one man who's a magistrate – and many an Oxford scholar keen to lose his virginity!' She began to laugh. 'They know where their member is, but don't know what to do with it. Why, a young gent I had a few weeks back was so scared he was struck silent the whole time and could scarce e'en manage to thank me after.'

I looked at her, marvelling. 'But . . . but do you not continually find yourself in a certain condition?'

She shook her head. 'I do not, for there are secrets to the game which are known to all ladies of the night.'

'And what are these?'

'I take a daily cordial of tansy and pennyroyal, which I was told to do by a mountebank in London to keep my terms regular,' she confided. 'As well as that, one or two of my regular gents, not wishing to find themselves with bastards to despoil their family names, have taken to wearing a device made from a pig's bladder which they wear over their member.'

I blushed to hear such talk, although wished that Master Geoffrey could have used such a device.

'But if you are not to try for a gent'man yourself, then we must endeavour to improve your position here. Do you have any money?'

I nodded and, trusting her completely, for she had been so open with me, brought out from my pocket the fold of paper which Mr Peakes had given me the day before.

Only one day before, I thought in disbelief, I'd bade good-bye to my fellow servants in Dun's Tew and heard John Taylor's voice for the last time. Thinking on this, a pretty conceit formed in my head: that if, on hearing him speak, I'd revealed myself in the back of the cart and asked for his aid, then perhaps he would have reached into the cart to rescue me. He might have struck off my leg irons on his anvil, thrown me over a horse and carried me away to safety.

I felt my eyes fill with tears at this sentimental and silly notion and Rebecca had to shake my arm gently to stir me. 'How much money have you there?' she asked, and when we counted it, found that there was three shillings and four pence.

'You are a made woman!' she said. 'With this you can send out for some warm things, hire a mattress, buy some better food and even have a little tipple of brandy to warm you of an evening. And what clothes have you?'

I unrolled my bundle and showed her, and her eyes rounded in admiration at the sight of the bodice, which she offered to sell for me. I turned her down, however, for I felt I had riches enough with my three shillings and fourpence, and should keep the bodice for another occasion. 'You must guard that, for it's worth a deal of money,' she said. 'And when you need to sell it I'll get you a good price.'

I thanked her kindly and said I would remember her words, and she offered to go and speak to the turnkeys and bargain with them for whatever I wanted. We debated how I should spend my money, and I was happy to discover that I'd be able to hire a mattress stuffed with straw, a pair of fur gloves and a woollen tippet, some candles and a candle-stick, and still have enough over to buy food for several days. Another discussion led to us deciding that I'd dine later that day on oysters and boiled ham, and of course I invited her to share these delicacies with me. I felt a good deal better while these discussions were going on for, although still cold and frightened, I was very content that my situation would shortly improve.

I waited while Rebecca went to speak first to the turnkeys and then – for she sent a message to say so – to the prison bailiff to pay what was owed and to organize the delivery of some of the items. She warned me that she drove a hard bargain so this could take some time, but said she'd be back well before midday and hoped to have the boiled ham with her. She suggested that we have a couple of measures of spiced wine with it in order to heat our bellies, and I thought this a most agreeable proposal.

It was about midday when a turnkey brought the bread, but Rebecca hadn't returned. It got later and later, and as I sat watching the darkness creep down the walls, it finally dawned on me that she wasn't going to come back at all. I'd been cheated out of my money! I'd been taken for a fool and Rebecca – or whatever her real name might be – was probably even now in one of the private rooms upstairs, drinking a toast to her good fortune.

Later that evening I spoke to a watchman and tried to make a complaint against her, only to discover that she was not a prisoner at all, but a well-known trickster who would bribe a turnkey now and again to let her into the gaol so that she might prey on gullible newcomers.

I spent that night in devastating loneliness, for I felt that I had not a friend in the world and might die of cold, hunger and misery and no one would care. I thought of my ma and pa, and my sister Jane and my brothers, and wondered what they were all doing; how they would have heard the news and what they thought of me. In that very low time I felt that even they had forsaken me.

I was woken – for I eventually slept, despite everything

– by someone shaking my shoulder. Opening my eyes, I found my sister standing beside me holding her nose, her face horror-struck at the surroundings in which she found herself. For a moment I thought that I must be dreaming, but then I looked past her and saw my ma there, too, looking around, as frightened as a fawn, and immediately jumped up and threw myself upon them, hugging them both.

We wept many tears together, and Jane and Ma could not desist from looking about them and shuddering and bewailing my situation, and saying how could I stand it and that I'd surely run mad in such a place. And while they were speaking, a prisoner was relieving himself in the kennel, another was gnawing at a dead rat, the man who stood on his head was happily doing so again, and yet another, covered in sores, was skipping around naked – so that it did indeed look like Bedlam and I was dreadfully ashamed to have caused Ma and Jane to come there.

They told me they'd started off from Steeple Barton on Farmer Smith's turnip cart at three o'clock that morning and my poor dear mother, exhausted from the journey and the shock, looked as though she'd aged twenty years. They wanted to know all that had happened to me, and what was expected to happen, and this I told them and could not hold back my tears as I did so, being so very thankful to have them there.

'But who will speak up for you at the trial?' Ma asked, after I'd told them all.

I said I didn't know.

'Should you not have someone on your side, to give their opinion of you?' asked Jane.

Ma nodded. 'Or otherwise Sir Thomas will have it all his own way, and he, being a man of the law, will take his advantage.'

I thought for a moment. 'But 'twill be known from the size of the babe that 'twas not full-term. And the gentlemen of the jury will be on my side, for they'll discern that I was telling the truth and surely feel pity for someone so deceived.'

'But as you said, they are *gentlemen* of the jury,' Ma said, 'landed gentry all, and probably kin to Sir Thomas for all we know. They will naturally be on his side, Anne, for they are of his persuasion.'

I frowned, thinking on this.

'And just suppose . . .' she went on with a tremor in her voice, 'you *are* found guilty, what then?'

'But I will not be – for I didn't kill the child!' I said, 'and even if the jury should go against me, then surely the judge will not.'

Ma said nothing more, but turned away and could not speak.

Sadly, they only had an hour with me while Farmer Smith took his turnips to the market and then came to collect them from the prison for their return, but before they left, Jane gave me seven pence, which I knew was all her savings, and Ma gave me a whole chicken which she'd roasted on the spit the previous day, and also two silver shillings.

''Tis from your father and 'tis his cow money, Anne, so use it well,' she said, pressing it into my hand. This was the first word I'd had of my father, for I'd been scared to ask after him in case he'd disowned me, and hearing now that he'd sent me his precious cow money touched me deeply.

I took them both to the iron door of the prison, where we said our goodbyes, and they promised to visit me again before the trial. They wept pitifully as they left, and so did I, for to see them going off into the freezing fog of the morning, knowing I was the cause of all their sorrows, fair broke my heart.

CHAPTER EIGHTEEN

Robert turned to a new section of his notebook and wrote:

> *Saturday, 14th December 1650*
> *11.15 a.m. – The dissection of the body of Anne Green was*
> *halted on her eye being seen to move by several of*
> *the assembled scholars.*

He looked at this note and then changed the word *eye* to *eyelid*, for Dr Petty was known to be a pedant for precise language.

Having decided to bleed their patient, the doctors sent for a bowl and tourniquet; as, providentially, they were working above an apothecary's shop, these items were located just down the stairs. Martha was also called upon to obtain some extra candles and two large cushions, these latter enabling the corpse to be placed in a semi-upright position.

Anne Green, reclining on pillows, looked less like a cadaver and more like a person – though the trembling of her eyelid had ceased and there was absolutely no animation about her at all. Robert glanced out of the window at the mob; he was sure he could see Anne's mother. How utterly bewildered she'd be to see Anne sitting up and being bled, just as if she were alive.

And perhaps, by fair means or foul, she *was* alive.

His heart quickened as he thought of foul means, for a horrifying thought had just occurred to him: maybe Anne Green was a witch. Maybe she had foiled the hangman and secured her life by the use of magick – and without stopping to consider the soundness of such an action his eyes moved over her body looking for teats at which a familiar might have suckled.

He could see none. And then he scolded himself, for this was the middle of the seventeenth century and he was a student at the most forward-thinking institute for learning in the country. A mere five years ago, the Puritan Matthew Hopkins had instituted witch hunts all over the rural south-east and been instrumental in the hanging of nearly 300 alleged witches, but Hopkins had since been discredited – and they were now, surely, living in more enlightened times, when a woman might grow old and bent without being accused of consorting with the Devil. Besides, the comely person of Anne Green did not in any way fit that description.

Dr Willis applied a tourniquet just below Anne's shoulder. This was tightened, a small incision made in her fleshy upper arm and the bleeding bowl held underneath.

A short moment passed, during which time everyone in the room held their breath, then a drop of blood was seen at the site of the cut. This grew larger, then formed into a ragged line which slowly trickled down Anne's arm and into the bowl beneath. Wren let out a cheer echoed by several of the other scholars, and Robert wrote with shaking hand:

11.20 a.m. – Anne Green's arm was lanced and she was seen to give blood to an approximate amount of

'Not so fast with your cheering, boys,' Dr Bathurst said. 'I have seen dead corpses bleed before now.'

Wilton frowned and asked, 'Is it true, sir, that a corpse bleeds when it is in the presence of its killer?' and just then – at that precise moment – Sir Thomas strode into the room at the head of a small party consisting of the Puritan, Mr Stegg the prison governor, a legal scribe and a uniformed sergeant-at-arms. There was a murmur of astonishment from the rest of the room, loaded glances were exchanged and the scholars shuffled round to allow the new party access to the corpse.

'Are you bleeding her, Dr Willis?' asked the scribe,

surveying the body on the table with amazement. 'How so? Since when does one bleed a dead corpse?'

'When one suspects she may not be entirely dead,' Dr Willis answered, with scarcely a glance at the deputation.

'You must stop this nonsense at once,' said Sir Thomas. 'Tell them, Stegg! Order them to stop.'

Mr Stegg scratched his head but no one else moved. Every person present continued to stare at Anne's arm as her life blood, its colour showing bright in the dull-hued room, trickled into the metal bowl until it was a quarter full. A strip of linen was then wrapped around her arm and the bleeding stopped.

Robert wrote *approximately five fluid ounces* in the space left in his notes.

'I think we will apply a clyster next!' Dr Petty said with some levity to his voice. 'This will bring heat and warmth to her bowels and may have some significant effect.'

'Dammit, sir, I tell you that you will *not* do such a thing!' Sir Thomas shouted. He gestured around at the prison officials. 'Can't someone stop all this? What does a person have to do to make this madness cease?'

The Puritan stepped forward. 'The very idea that you should attempt to raise the dead is improper and profane.' He extended his arms in preacherly pose. 'Every man and woman has a time to be born and a time to die. It is not meet to interfere with the holy scheme of things. Man should not be raised again.'

Dr Willis looked at him keenly. 'What of the raising of Lazarus? His time to die had come, but Jesus raised him up once more.'

'Do you dare to compare your works to those of the Lord, sir?'

'I believe the Lord said afterwards that Lazarus had merely been sleeping,' Mr Clarke said and, over an anguished cry of 'Blasphemy!' from the Puritan, hurriedly addressed Dr Petty: 'What do you require for the clyster, sir? I shall go downstairs and obtain whatever's necessary.'

'Something mild. Hot rainwater, perhaps, with a little pepper or warming spices in it?' Dr Petty mused. 'What think you, Thomas?'

Dr Willis nodded his agreement. 'And – while you're in your stock cupboard, John – perhaps we should have some cantharides to try and produce blistering.'

As Mr Clarke went off, Dr Petty put his fingers to the neck of Anne Green and felt around for a pulse. 'Perhaps . . . perhaps . . .' he said, shaking his head doubtfully. 'Though if I feel anything, it is so faint as to hardly be there at all.'

Robert wrote: *11.30 a.m. – Faint pulse?*

'Observe the colour of her face, however,' Dr Petty

suddenly said with some excitement, studying Anne's cheeks closely. 'She grows pinker, surely . . .'

'Damn you for your ignorance!' Sir Thomas shouted, making everyone start. 'Am I to understand that you are going to act outside the law and will continue to try and resurrect this woman?'

'Yes,' said Dr Petty curtly. 'And 'twould be better if you just left us to it and stopped causing these constant interruptions.'

'Please remember, sir, that these rooms are our domain,' said Dr Willis.

'But the law is mine!'

Footsteps sounded along the corridor and two fellows of Christ Church ran into the room. They had dressed hurriedly, for one was without his gown and the other was still struggling into his at the door.

'We have heard the rumour!' the first said.

'Is it true?'

'Does the hanged woman truly live?' asked the first with incredulity. 'There are whispers of it about the quad.'

The face of Sir Thomas showed total rage. 'See what's happening? All and sundry will prattle of this and 'twill become a freak show! You are using this woman for your own ends.'

'Not so, sir,' Dr Petty said mildly.

'You are using her to endeavour to increase your fortune!'

This last remark was ignored and the two new fellows took their places around the body of Anne Green, staring at her with a still and silent absorption.

'Her feet are extreme cold,' Dr Bathurst said to his fellows. 'While the clyster is being prepared perhaps we could anoint them with spirit of turpentine. 'Twill make the skin hot and she may feel the benefit.'

'Indeed.' Dr Willis nodded. 'And her legs and arms should be rubbed to increase the circulation of her blood to her extremities.'

'Very well,' Sir Thomas suddenly roared, 'then let her live!'

At this strange and unexpected change of heart the medical men turned to stare at him.

'And as soon as she is on her feet – nay, as soon as she can answer to her rightful name – then I will see to it that she is taken back to the prison yard and re-hanged. And this time I will personally ensure that the matter is carried out with no opportunity for error. Even if I have to knot the rope and push her off the damned gibbet myself!'

There was a pause and then Dr Petty corrected him. 'You will *not* take her, sir.'

'For we shall see that you do not,' said Dr Willis. 'And if

by some miracle we do cause her to live again, and she thrives, then we shall put her on the witness stand and all shall hear the truth of it: the reason why, when a woman has clearly miscarried a child which was but nine inches long, she should be found guilty of murder.'

Sir Thomas seemed about to say something else, but then choked on his words and clutched at his chest. For several moments he seemed to find it difficult to draw breath, and although Dr Petty called for a chair to be brought so that he might examine him, Sir Thomas would have none of it. 'None . . . none . . . of you bloody quacks here will lay a finger on me!' he croaked, backing away.

Dr Petty bowed. 'As you wish, sir.'

'Do not think I shall allow you continue with this,' Sir Thomas railed when he had gathered a little more strength. 'I shall return here with greater authority . . . I shall call upon Cromwell himself to judge whether this . . . this profane act should be . . . be . . .'

But he had gone a strange yellow colour – as yellow as his teeth, someone was later to report – and seemed to find it difficult to say more. He backed out of the room, his feet shuffling as if he could barely move them along the ground, his eyes always on Anne Green. The Puritan, protesting once more that the revival of corpses was ungodly work, left at the same time, supporting Sir Thomas on his slow progress down the corridor.

Mr Stegg, the prison governor, approached the doctors with deference, for Dr Petty had, earlier that year, saved his wife from choking to death on a cherry stone. 'Good gentlemen all, I feel this is none of my business,' he said expansively. 'The girl was hanged, she was dead and there's an end to it. What happens now is naught to do with me.'

'Wise words, sir,' Dr Willis said, giving him a short bow from the other side of the body.

'So if you'll excuse me, I'll return to my duties.' Nudging the scribe, he gave a bow towards the doctors and both men turned away.

'But hold one moment,' Dr Willis said. 'If you wish to co-operate with the Divine Providence that may have saved this woman, then perhaps you would do so by contacting the court usher and asking him that a reprieve may be granted until such time as she is recovered – if this be God's will – and an official pardon obtained for her.'

The scribe nodded. 'At your service, sir. I'll do it myself,' he added as he left the room, for he had fallen foul of Sir Thomas's temper in the past and was pleased to have this occasion to thwart him.

Spirit of turpentine was applied to the soles of Anne's feet and these, and her arms and legs, were rubbed vigorously. In spite of each of the doctors by turn using considerable energy to try and ignite a warmth, however, her feet and limbs remained as if frozen.

The students fell back, disappointed. Robert wrote:

> *11.45 a.m. – Anne Green's feet were painted with turpentine and her legs and arms rubbed with vigour. These attentions did not appear to make any difference.*

The enema was mixed and applied.

> *12 noon – A clyster of hot rainwater and spices was applied to the bowels of Anne Green to endeavour to increase the warmth of her privities. She gave no reaction.*

Dr Petty gave a cry of exasperation. 'We must have definite proof she is alive – and quickly!'

'Quite so,' said Dr Willis, 'or I fear Sir Thomas, on recovering from his ague, will use his influence to have her taken out of our care.'

Dr Bathurst approached the corpse and took up her hand. 'Anne Green!' he called urgently. 'Anne! Do you hear us?

'Can you speak?' asked Mr Clarke.

'Give a sign that you are alive – squeeze my hand or open your eyes!' urged Dr Petty.

There was no reaction.

12.20 p.m. – She was called to know whether she could either hear or speak. She did not move her hand nor open her eye to command, however.

'What do you say to giving her a cordial?' asked Dr Petty.

Dr Willis nodded eagerly. 'One with restorative properties.'

'Barley julep?' suggested Mr Clarke, and this was obtained.

12.25 a.m. – Drs Petty and Willis, by gradual force, unclenched Anne Green's teeth. A quantity of barley julep was poured down her throat but the swallowing action could not be produced and most of the liquid was seen to run out the sides of her mouth.

The doctors and students observed this solemnly and in silence. Robert felt himself to be quite ill with disappointment.

Three fellows of Brasenose appeared, bristling with curiosity, having heard of what was going on. Nineteen people were now crowded into the room, not including the corpse.

'She does not hear us and she does not swallow,' said Dr Willis with a sigh. 'She appears to have no reflexes at all. What now?'

There was another long silence. 'Perhaps the signs of life we observed were mere reactions of the nerves after death,' said Dr Bathurst somewhat reluctantly.

The others shook their heads unknowingly, then Mr Clarke suddenly clicked his fingers together and dashed out of the room. He returned a moment later with a long quill feather.

'She is to mark her name?' Dr Petty asked with an effort at a smile.

Mr Clarke shook his head, holding the quill aloft. 'One last thing to try . . . with your permission . . .'

Understanding what he meant, Drs Bathurst and Willis between them managed to unclench Anne Green's teeth once more, and the long feather was inserted to tickle the back of her throat.

As one, the scholars and doctors leaned forward and held their breath. For a moment nothing happened, and then her limp body suddenly convulsed with a cough.

A thrill of excitement ran around the room.

'Again!' urged Dr Willis, and the feather was inserted once more to the same effect.

There were some gasps, several cheers, and muted applause from a dozen pairs of gloved hands.

Robert, his hand shaking with excitement, wrote:

> *12.30 p.m. – Mr Clarke obtained a feather. Anne Green's teeth were unclenched and the back of her throat stimulated. She coughed twice.*

Let her live on, Robert thought to himself. She *must* live . . .

CHAPTER NINETEEN

What a short story mine seems, for it's as though only minutes have passed since I awoke into this strange state. I've tried, several times, to see the angels again, to open my eyes (or to somehow see them, miraculously, through my eyelids) and feel the comfort of their presence in the black which surrounds me, but they do not appear. I wonder now if I merely invented them to be a comfort to my troubled mind.

I survived my time in Oxford gaol because I truly believed that I only had to endure a certain number of days before the judge arrived and discovered me innocent.

I was prepared for the fact that I might be charged with fornication and was also prepared – indeed, almost willing – to take my chastisement for this, whether it was to be ducked, put into the stocks or whipped behind a cart. After I'd endured this, I thought, then I'd endeavour to put the terrors I'd suffered behind me. I'd go home and live quietly with Ma and Pa until I was no longer a subject of gossip, then try to obtain a position as a laundress or glove maker so that I wouldn't be a burden to them. I'd find work in my own village if I could, for I didn't ever intend to go into service in a big house again. *Hold the family you work for in high regard*, I'd been told throughout my life. *Obey your master with singleness of heart, for a good master will care for you like your own father*. But who'd ever cared about me there, in the Reade household?

And one day, perhaps – or so I still dreamed – a kind young man might come along I could trust, and I'd tell him all that had happened and he'd still want to marry me. I tried not to think too much about this, however, for in my heart I couldn't believe that a good and true man would ever want me, and that as certain as the wolf is in the dog, he'd flee when he got breath of the ill-luck and scandal that had been visited upon me.

Ma and Jane came to visit me again and, arriving on a day when my spirits were at a particularly low ebb, were able to cheer me somewhat. They brought some fresh bread with them, and a whole cheese and some cooked potatoes, and Jane also brought two pretty combs for my hair and a wash ball she'd made herself from pink soapwort, and these dainty things thrilled my heart. They brought news from home, too, for Bramble and Bracken were due to lamb after Christmas, and told me that the chickens had been frighted by a fox and had stopped laying; also that the cunning woman had treated Jacob Twister for a growth in his stomach and cured him completely (although I could not but show some disbelief at this). I listened eagerly to these stories of the outside world but, once told, they flitted through my head like shadows, none seeming true or real. My only reality was the gaol and getting through my time within it, minute by foul minute.

Every day I asked the turnkeys the date, and as it crept so slowly toward the thirteenth I tried to temper my impatience, telling myself that the judge might have been held up on his journey and that I'd only had *her* – the whore's – word for when he was due. That very day, however, on Friday the thirteenth day of December, we prisoners were roused early in the morning and the turnkeys spread the word that on this day the judge would hear the cases of those of us who'd not yet been charged.

After we'd eaten the foul slop that passed for breakfast Mr Stegg, the prison governor, came down and read out some twenty names, including mine, and those called were herded and manacled together and presently led in a staggering, ragged procession out of the door I'd entered through two weeks before. This was the first time I'd been outside in all those days and, dazzled by the light, I wanted to stand and look about me and breathe in the fresh frosty air. I dared not pause for more than a moment, however, or would have found myself upturned and dragged along by the others. I had just a few seconds to stare at the sky, and saw it was very soft and grey, tinged with pink, and the clouds drawn across it seemed like thin, translucent silk. There was but one tree to be seen, and although this was without leaves, frost had rimed its upper branches so that it sparkled in the chill air. And indeed everything about that small view of the world seemed different and heightened and beautiful after the darkness and stench of the gaol.

We were taken across a mound of grass white with hoarfrost and then led to another part of the castle where the court was to meet, into a dim space named an ante-room. The judge was breakfasting, we were told by a man called an usher, and when he'd eaten and drunk all he wanted, then he would hear our cases. There was a wit among us by the name of Michael Lee, a footpad, small and shrunken and eaten up with scurvy, who, on hearing this, threw a shilling across to the usher and asked him to go and buy a decent bottle of brandy for the judge to have with his breakfast, for he would as soon have him merry as sober.

We waited a goodly time and there was not much talk-ing amongst us for, whether it was our first time or no, we were all afeared of what punishment we might receive and whether this might be accomplished quickly so that we could be out of gaol for Christmas.

Michael Lee was called first. His irons were knocked off so that he was no longer chained to the rest of us, and he was pushed up the stairs which led to the court room. He was only there about ten minutes when we heard a faint roar and some applause, and then he was pushed back into our room and manacled again.

We asked him how he'd fared, and he replied pretty well, for he'd been sentenced to be branded on the cheek and professed he was content with this, for it was his third offence and he might have been hanged. He was more troubled than he cared to admit, however, and touched his cheek over and over, muttering that it was nothing at all, 'twould be over very quickly, he would make sure he was in his cups so wouldn't feel a thing, and so on. In the end the others told him to quiet his mouth.

Another man went in then, accused of fraud. Found guilty, he was sentenced to be sent to the Americas. An old widow woman was next, and came back weeping, saying she'd been ordered to stay in the prison until someone paid the money she owed her grocer, which was three shillings, and she felt she might never see her home again.

There came another wait, and those of us who had not yet been called were a-twitching with the worry of it all.

While we waited I tidied my hair back as best I could with the combs that Jane had given me (although it felt lank and foul and was running with fleas), and tried to rub some spots of dirt from my gown, for I didn't want to appear frowsy and lackadaisical. *Cleanliness is next to Godliness*, it says in a text on the wall of the dairy, which was sewn by Lady Mary's own hand. If I looked clean, I wondered, would I appear more innocent? Was a maid who wore grimy clothes more likely to have killed her own babe?

At last an usher of the court came and called, 'Anne Green!' in a loud voice, and, although I had been waiting and looking forward to this moment for many days, when I heard that call of my name I felt a coldness and a terror go through me and became extreme afraid.

My manacles were struck off and I'd just a moment to rub the smarting places on my legs where the bracelets had rubbed and blistered before I was pushed up the stairs by a uniformed sergeant-at-arms, who then followed me up and stood behind me all the while to prevent my escape.

My first impression of the courtroom was that we were in a church, for it was a tall and well-ordered space, with dark wooden panelling and windows all round. In this room were a great many seats and benches, and on these a number of people were seated. I've seen pictures of a play performed in a theatre and it reminded me something of this, for although the seats were at different angles, they faced towards one thing, and that thing was the little wooden box in which I was standing.

My legs were light and frail without the irons on them, and such was my apprehension of what was to come that I felt myself swaying and had to grip the edge of the box in order to stay upright. Once steady, I began hesitantly to look around me and saw, to my great horror, Sir Thomas and Lady Reade sitting very close and both staring at me with stone-cold eyes. Behind them the people seemed all of a blur, for my eyes were out of sorts having so much light after so long. I saw several of my fellow servants from the house, however, and my dear ma and pa dressed in their Sunday best, and my two brothers who must have come from Banbury, and others whom I could not concentrate on or give name to just then, for I felt light in the head and full of wonder as to how I had ended up there.

To my right were seated two rows of gentlemen I took to be the jury, looking pompous and severe enough to make me tremble anew, and several legal gentlemen in wigs and gowns, and a lot more, I think, from the university, some with purple gowns, and some younger men who were perhaps scholars, with black gowns over their suits and an air of anticipation about them.

And all there to see me.

I began to sway and might have fallen if the sergeant-at-arms had not gripped my arm firmly, telling me in a harsh voice to keep my place. A man in a steel-coloured wig, who was named Dr Grey, then stood up and began to speak. He asked my name and where I was born and I told him, but I had to repeat this twice more, for he said he could barely hear me. And as I spoke, everything I said was written down by two scribes, who were sitting on low seats scribbling and scratching away with their quill pens.

I was asked to swear on the Holy Bible that I would speak the absolute truth, so help me God, which I did, and someone addressed me crossly, saying that I really must speak louder or they could not proceed, and when I looked up to where the voice had come from I saw the judge for the first time. He was in velvet robes with fur at the edges and had a great waved mane of white hair. I found out later that his name was Judge Unton Croke, although I had to call him 'my lord' whenever I addressed him.

Dr Grey called the names of the men of the jury one by one, and said they were all gentlemen and would stand as jurors for his highness Oliver Cromwell, Lord Protector of the Commonwealth of England, Scotland and Ireland, and I looked around fearfully in case he should be there too, but it did not appear that he was. After calling out their names, Dr Grey said that I could object to any of the jury if I wished, but I didn't really understand what was meant by this, so said to him that I thought they'd do well enough, thank you kindly.

Someone stood, unrolled a parchment and read out the charge against me, which was that on the first day of December in the year of Our Lord 1650 I had sought to cover the sin of fornication with a greater sin, namely I had most unnaturally and barbarously murdered my child so that it would not be discovered that I had conceived a bastard. And he asked if I pleaded guilty to this charge, or not guilty.

And I said not guilty, and he corrected me, 'Not guilty, *my lord*,' and I repeated this.

And then things began to happen very quickly, for various people stood up in the courtroom and said different things, some of which I didn't understand, and others went into another wooden box similar to mine and were spoken to by Dr Grey or the judge and asked questions. And at some time I was asked by Dr Grey if I'd known all along that I was with child.

I said that yes, I had thought that I was, and he then enquired how long it had been since my courses had ceased. This question embarrassed me somewhat, but I replied as sensibly as I could that I thought they had ceased about five or six months previous to my giving birth. Dr Grey wanted to know if I'd informed my employers of my condition so that arrangements could be made for my lying-in, and I said I had not. And when he heard this he said I had therefore concealed my condition from the world.

I began to weep and said I had not, for I had told my mother, and also told the father of the child.

'And who is the father?' asked Dr Grey.

I took a breath and was about answer up with the name of Master Geoffrey when Sir Thomas stood up.

'I object,' he said, 'for how is the naming of the father of this poor dead infant relevant to this case?'

Dr Grey said, 'It may be – for perhaps the father of it had a hand in its demise.'

'But whatever she says, this girl's word cannot be believed. Being caught out in her foul deed, she may name someone out of spite.'

'But I say it may be a way of discerning her intentions,' Dr Grey said. 'Was she about to be married to the man in question, perhaps?'

'She was not,' Sir Thomas said. 'And besides, she is nothing but a lying whore and always has been!'

I'm pleased to recall that there was a gasp of horror across the court at these spiteful words, and Sir Thomas was told to apologize to the judge for uttering them. He did so, but grudgingly, and I felt very much disquieted after.

I was asked about my travail in the house of office and how long I'd stayed there, and also if I'd picked up the child after I'd birthed it and tried to aid its breathing in any way.

I hesitated, longing to say that I had done something to help it but, remembering that I was on an oath to speak the truth, did not dare. 'The child was pale and still,' I replied haltingly, 'and made neither sound nor movement, so I did not touch it.'

'But how did you know without a shadow of doubt that it was dead?' the judge asked me.

'I knew it, my lord, for it was too small to have ever lived,' I said, and these simple words sounded strange and unnatural to my own ears, and I began to be afeared that no one would believe me.

A midwife was brought up to the stand who said she'd been working for seventeen years and had attended hundreds of births, and they asked if she'd examined the body of my dead babe and what was her opinion of it. I held my breath here and could not look at her for fear of what she was going to say, but to my relief she answered up with conviction that in her opinion the child was not viable, for it was but nine inches long and hardly formed.

'It was formed enough for it to be seen that it was a male child, however,' Dr Grey pointed out, and she admitted that this was correct. Someone else in the court asked if a certain test had been carried out to ascertain whether the lungs of the dead child had ever held air, and it was answered that it had not.

The midwife left the stand and the judge addressed me. 'Were you very frightened when you knew you were with child?' he asked.

'Yes, my lord.' I nodded. 'For I knew the punishments which could be afforded me.'

'So did you ever seek to rid yourself of the burden of it?'

I felt my cheeks flush.

'Remember that you have put your hand on the book containing God's word, and sworn to tell the truth before Him,' he warned.

I hung my head. 'Yes, I . . . I once took a cordial prescribed by a cunning woman,' I said, and heard a little stir in the court. He asked when this was, and I told him the truth of it.

'And – this cordial having not brought about the change you required, what arrangements did you make for your confinement?'

'I did not make any, my lord.'

'So it might be presumed from this that you did not ever intend the child to live?'

I heard a murmuring from the court.

'And that you sought to hide the sin of your fornication with the greater one of murder.'

'I never did, my lord!'

'But you admit the sin of the flesh?'

I nodded. 'But I was tricked into sinning with false promises!' I said, and thought again to give Master Geoffrey's name. When I looked up, however, I saw Sir Thomas glaring at me, shaking his head as much as to say, *You dare to say* . . . and I did not dare.

Next Sir Thomas went into the witness box to speak, and gave his name and a great list of all his titles, like Lord of the Manors of Beedon, Appleford, Barton and a great many other places, and said that he was granted MA at Middle Temple and had served as High Sheriff of Berkshire, Oxfordshire and elsewhere, and these accreditations went on for so long that I lost track of why we were being told of them. When he'd finished, Mr Grey asked if he was the employer of the accused, Anne Green, and what he thought of my character.

'She is a maid in my employ,' he said, 'but until recently I had no idea of what type of a woman she was.' Beside him, Lady Mary's eyes were closed as if she didn't want to see too much, and her hands clasped as if in prayer.

'And what sort of a woman is she, sir?' asked Dr Grey.

'The very lowest kind,' said Sir Thomas. 'I was shocked

and revolted to find that one of my own maidservants had been acting so lewdly, for I believed that I kept a Christian household.'

'Quite, sir,' said Dr Grey.

'But since that . . . that *woman* was arrested I've heard that she'd been making herself available to any man who came a-calling, whether he be barber, blacksmith or baker. She's brought shame upon my house and my good name with her loose and vulgar ways.'

'I have not been loose!' I cried out. 'Or only with one. And before I lay with him, I was unblemished.'

'So you say, madam,' said Sir Thomas dismissively.

'You may ask my fellow servants,' I said to the judge. 'Ask them of my character.'

The judge made a gesture towards the open court, as much as to say did anyone there want to speak for me, but there was naught but silence. I was sad at this, but with Sir Thomas standing in front so puffed up and haughty, which of them was going to speak and say well of me and be cast onto the streets for their pains? Besides, so solemn and daunting was the air of the court that a mere servant would hardly have dared get to his feet, let alone have spoken.

'Have you anything to say in mitigation?' Dr Grey asked me next, and I did not understand what this meant and must have looked a buffoon, for he added, 'Is there anything you want to say which might lessen your culpability? For instance, perhaps you overlaid the child, or stopped its breathing for just a moment because it was crying, and so by mistake it died.'

'I did not!' I answered indignantly.

He bowed to the judge. 'I therefore conclude the case.'

The judge spoke to the jury, telling them that they should now decide whether I spoke the truth or not, and they all got up and went into a huddle on the back bench, speaking together for ten minutes or so. And all this time I stood in the box hanging my head – for I could not look out upon those gathered there, and was scarce able to draw breath for the terror of my situation.

When at last the twelve men regained their seats, the nearest of their number stood up. I looked towards him, and as I did so there came a harsh cough from Sir Thomas and I swear that the juryman's eyes flickered towards his. The apprehension came to me then that all was not going to go well for me.

The juryman said, 'We have reached our verdict, my lord.'

'And is it the verdict of you all?' said the judge.

'It is.'

The judge asked, 'How do you find the defendant, Anne Green: guilty or not guilty of murder?'

'Guilty, my lord.'

There was a gasp in the room and I let the words settle into my brain. I recall screaming, then, ''Tis not true! May God be my witness I did not kill my child!' and I saw my mother on her feet, also crying out.

'Silence!' Dr Grey said.

'I will now pass sentence,' said the judge when all was quiet again, and there was a pause before a tiny sound crossed the room: no more than a soft intake of breath from all assembled there.

Bewildered to know what could have caused this, for he had not yet said what the sentence was, I looked to the judge and saw that he had placed a square of black silk foursquare upon his long white wig.

'Anne Green,' he said solemnly, 'you have been found guilty of infanticide – that is, the murder of your child – and I therefore sentence you to be taken to the castle yard and there hanged by the neck until dead.'

I stared ahead, uncomprehending.

'You should spend the rest of your time on this Earth praying for forgiveness for the monstrous sin you have committed, and may the Lord have mercy on your soul.'

The sergeant-at-arms beside me stepped forward and asked, 'When should the sentence be carried out, my lord?'

'Tomorrow morning at seven thirty,' the judge answered.

I looked at him blankly, for I could scarce understand what had been ordered.

'You are dismissed,' he said to me, and called for the next case to be brought in.

As the sergeant-at-arms pushed me towards the stairs I was aware of one more thing happening: of a smart gentleman wearing a long red silk waistcoat over a black cloak and with the tasselled cap of a learned man, standing and making a plea that my corpse, after hanging, should be granted to the medical department of the university so that it might be dissected for the furtherance of medical knowledge.

And I heard my mother's screams at this before I was pushed downstairs and re-shackled.

CHAPTER TWENTY

By one o'clock there were twenty-five people in the dissection room, and by one fifteen, thirty-one. All were male but for Anne Green, and the room was no longer cold, but stuffy, and smelled of moist wool cloaks, stale tobacco and damp hair. Everyone being hungry, a flagon of ale was sent for, and Martha, (who had only anticipated a dozen for dinner) appeared with woefully inadequate portions of bread, cheese and sliced meats and placed them on a folding butler's table in the corridor just outside the room. The doctors hoped that some of the onlookers might, on seeing the paucity of the food, go and take their dinner in the nearby Rainbow, but no one seemed inclined to do so.

Throughout this time, Robert continued with his note-taking.

12.45 p.m. – The patient was bled again and four ounces of blood flowed freely into the metal bowl.
12.55 p.m. – Her legs were bound with linen strips to try and encourage the flow of blood to them.

1.00 p.m. – The sore and bruised place on her neck (where rubbed by the hangman's noose) was oiled in order to soothe it.

1.15 p.m. – Her hands were chafed to warm and stimulate them.

1.25 p.m. – Hot stones were placed beneath her feet.

1.40 p.m. – A plaister of sheep dung and pitch was mixed and applied to her breast to endeavour to warm her heart.

Anne Green's response to all these attentions was to flutter her eyelids tremulously, but so quickly did this happen that those who were paying attention to another part of her body missed it. A pulse, however, had been detected by Dr Petty, who was said to have sensitive fingers, but not by Dr Willis. Dr Bathurst was undecided as to whether he could feel anything or not.

Robert recorded the ministrations carefully, willing her to live with every fibre of his being. He vowed to himself that she was not – could not be – guilty of murder.

A notice had been received from the offices of the prison granting the woman named Anne Green a temporary reprieve, and this had been nailed to the wall behind where they were working, in case Sir Thomas should try to remove her.

'If we *can* revive her, you know what this will do for Oxford, don't you?' Dr Willis said to Dr Petty. He spoke in a low voice but Robert, standing close by, was privy to their words.

'We will obtain more fresh corpses, perhaps,' came the answer. 'That will be an excellent good thing.'

Dr Willis nodded. 'But as well as that . . .'

Dr Petty didn't reply, for he was wondering whether to apply another plaister above Anne's heart and what materials should be used this time in its making.

'Why, people will flock here!' Dr Willis went on. 'Oxford will become a holy city. They'll make a shrine of the place!'

'They may.' Dr Petty nodded.

'They will! The people of England have passed through the abyss that was the Civil War and are looking for proof of God. This housemaid may be regarded as a messenger from Him, to prove His existence.'

On Dr Petty looking unmoved, he went on earnestly, 'William, this woman called on God to prove her innocence to the world. If she lives, then He has heard and saved her.'

Dr Petty smiled. 'Perhaps.'

'It can only be a most excellent thing for us!'

'Yes, this could make our reputations. If she survives,

then word will spread across the world of our success.'

'Our success through Christ,' Dr Willis reminded him piously. 'What we've done through His good graces.'

'But what,' Dr Bathurst interceded, 'if the girl persists in this present state; this condition where she seems neither fully dead nor completely alive?'

The medical men exchanged glances.

'For I have heard,' Dr Bathurst continued, 'of someone who slept for a hundred years and didn't speak or move in all that time.'

The other two smiled. 'That's but a fairy tale!' said Dr Petty.

'Well, perhaps not a hundred years, but a very great number,' Dr Bathurst assured them. 'He was in a trance or a sleep and couldn't be waked from it. About sixty years, I believe it was, before he finally died.'

'Well,' said Dr Willis, 'if this happens and Anne Green decides to play Sleeping Beauty with us, they will still flock to Oxford!' He paused. 'What if, though, she has no soul when she recovers? What if she is merely some form of wraith?'

The others exchanged further concerned looks but did not reply.

Robert, after being privy to these conversations and prompted by further calls from the crowd outside, prepared himself to speak by breathing in deeply several times. Rehearsing in his head what he was to say, and pointing first outside and then at Anne in order to illustrate his speech, he asked, 'M . . . m . . . m . . . mother?'

'She is not a mother,' Dr Petty said, glancing at him. 'For that was the charge against her. That she had—'

Robert shook his head, pointed to Anne again and then outside. 'Her . . . her . . . her . . . m . . . m . . .' he said.

'I think he means her mother is outside waiting in this foul weather,' Dr Bathurst said.

'That's something we should think on,' said Dr Petty. 'Should we fetch the woman here? Should her family be witness to this miracle? This near-miracle,' he amended.

Robert nodded vehemently, concerned about Anne's family, but almost as anxious about her opening her eyes and finding herself on a dissection table surrounded by doctors wearing bloodied aprons and wielding instruments, with ne'er a familiar face near.

'I say they shouldn't come in yet,' Dr Willis said, after thinking a moment. 'Suppose she doesn't survive? It would be cruel to raise hopes that might well prove unfounded.'

Dr Bathurst lowered his voice slightly. 'And suppose she lives, but runs mad? What then?'

'Indeed.' Dr Petty sighed as he considered this. 'We must remember that her family will only be simple folk and this may be more than they can comprehend.'

Dr Willis nodded. 'They've seen her hanged and pronounced dead . . . and then to find that she is suddenly not dead . . .'

'They will think her an angel!' said Dr Bathurst.

''Tis enough to make even a wise man consider his sanity,' said Dr Petty. He turned to Robert. 'Perhaps we should keep things within this room for now, and then tomorrow morning, if she still lives . . .'

'They'll continue waiting outside,' Dr Bathurst said. 'They'll wait there until they receive what remains of her.'

Robert felt a stab of disappointment. He'd wanted to – not, alas, tell the family himself – but to witness them being told. He'd wanted to share their joy.

'Tomorrow,' Dr Willis said to Robert, and he nodded.

A man wearing black entered the room. He was elaborately dressed, however, and his tall hat was decorated with braid, loops of ribbon and a gold buckle, so it was immediately apparent that he had no truck with the Puritans.

'Is it true?' he was heard to say excitedly as he squeezed through the crowd. 'Is it really true? They're talking about it all over.'

''Tis true – but get to the back,' someone called to him.

'And there's no room to wear that hat in here!'

The doctors looked at each other. 'And as for the news staying within the room . . .' remarked Dr Petty with some irony.

It was eight o'clock that evening when the doctors finally packed up their instruments. The mob waiting in the street had dwindled, so they'd been told, to a core of about eight, and these few had obtained a covered cart from somewhere and settled themselves in it for the night, prepared to wait as long as they had to to obtain Anne's remains and give them a Christian burial.

Anne Green had been put through every medical procedure known to man, and had neither fully come round, nor declined further. Her heart was beating more strongly, certainly, for each doctor had now felt a pulse at her wrist and throat. Various cordials had been poured into her mouth, her face was pinker and appeared more swollen, her throat had turned blue and purple with bruising and traces of sweat had appeared under her arms. As a crowning proof, a small mirror had been obtained and Anne's breath had clouded it as evidence of air within her. In total, forty-six people had passed through the dissection room. Now all except the doctors, Christopher Wren and Robert had gone home.

As he folded up his notebook Robert looked out of the window at the cart, its canvas covering showing the soft glow of candlelight within, and wondered if any news of Anne had reached her family. The next morning, assuming that she still lived, he intended to be there when they were told.

But first they had to get her through the night.

'She ought to be moved to a proper bed,' Dr Petty said. 'How can she get a good night's sleep on a dissection table?'

'She should certainly be kept as warm as possible overnight,' Dr Willis said. 'If she's allowed to get cold again it may undo all the good we've done.'

At that moment Martha came in collecting beakers and bowls. She was yawning widely, for her day had started at five that morning and she wanted to go to her bed. Dr Petty's eyes fell on her and he addressed Mr Clarke.

'Your maid,' he asked, 'does she live on the premises?'

Mr Clarke nodded. 'She has a small room at the end of the corridor.'

'With her own bed?'

'Indeed,' came the startled reply.

'Would she mind . . . ?' began Dr Petty, then whispered the rest of the sentence in the apothecary's ear. Mr Clarke shrugged; he appeared doubtful.

Nevertheless, a gently appeasing expression spread

over Dr Petty's face. 'Martha,' he began tentatively, 'we have it in mind to give you a bedfellow.'

Martha's jaw dropped. She'd been propositioned several times by scholars, but never by one of the doctors. And never in so open a fashion.

'Well, sir . . .' she began, blushing.

'No, fear not, not that!' said Dr Petty hastily. 'We are anxious for our patient here, and want to make sure she stays warm overnight. We wondered if we could prevail upon you to—'

Martha gave a short scream. 'Never! What – lie with a dead corpse?'

'She's not dead,' Wren said gently. 'Merely . . . sleeping.'

'You can be of *great* help to us,' said Dr Petty. 'It may make all the difference to whether she lives or dies.'

'When this case is being written of in the annals of medical history, then your name will be mentioned as being of particular significance,' said Dr Willis.

'And we will see to it that you receive the sum of five shillings,' added Dr Petty.

Robert looked at Martha's face and saw her expression falter and waver, going from fear and near-tearfulness to a kind of reluctant eagerness. 'What would I have to do?' she asked.

'Keep her warm, that's all.'

'Perhaps sleep with an arm about her.'

'If you could manage to rub her limbs a little . . .'

Martha gulped and nodded. 'I'll try, sirs,' she said. 'I'll try.'

CHAPTER TWENTY-ONE

As I go over these remembrances in my head I seem to hear the low murmur of voices. Is it a conversation, or one person on his own? Certainly I can hear a man's voice. Am I then nearing the gates of Heaven? Perhaps St Peter is approaching offering blessings – or perhaps 'tis the Devil, come to seek his own. But I am innocent! The Devil will surely know this and dare not take me.

The low murmuring ceases and I immediately lose the sense of when I heard it. A moment ago? Ten years past? Did I imagine or dream it?

But my life is almost told and I bring myself back to my last day on Earth, where, early in the morning, I sat on a stool in the condemned cell, my hands reaching towards a few sticks burning in the grate. The flames that rose from these glittered as merry and bright as flames always do, for they didn't know that they were burning in the room of one whose last moments were approaching, one who would shortly be hanged by the neck until dead.

I'd dismissed the cleric who wanted to save my soul,

for he and I had fallen to disagreement over my refusal to confess I was guilty of murder, or to ask God's forgiveness for such a thing. He'd insisted that judge and jury had found me guilty, and I'd insisted that, nevertheless, I had not committed any such crime. In the end, frustrated almost to the point of tears at my stubbornness, he had left, saying he'd return the next morning to accompany me to the prison yard, for the sight of the scaffold led many an obstinate person to confess their wickedness and, at the last, throw themselves on God's mercy.

I had asked for a fire to be built in my cell, which was granted to me as my last wish, and sat before it going over my life, as I do now in this black and eerie netherworld in which I find myself. And I wondered then – and wonder still – on the strangeness of life, and how the circumstances had occurred which led to my downfall, and if they might have been avoided by my having had a natal chart cast (as I've heard that the gentry do) showing what harsh planets were overhead. I might then have anticipated my coming disgrace and perhaps prevented such a thing.

During that long night I didn't feel so much affrighted as weary and disbelieving, for it seemed that I must have some part in a mummers play or be acting out a ballad. Surely 'twas not possible that I was in gaol and condemned to hang on the morrow? Where had my life fled? How had it happened so?

At six o'clock a turnkey came in with my breakfast, which, as it was my last, was red herrings, anchovies and fresh-baked bread. I felt hungry and was pleased to see such things, but as soon as I put them in my mouth they turned to ashes and refused to be swallowed, so I had to discard them.

At seven o'clock my sister, mother and father were allowed into my cell, and my heart leaped with joy to see them – but fell again as I remembered what they were there for. We wept and held each other, and it seemed to me the first time we had ever done such a thing, for we weren't a family given much to the linking of arms or the kissing of cheeks. Even my father shed tears, which made me exceedingly sorrowful.

My mother, who is ever a sensible woman, recovered first and said that I should now prepare myself and try to have as respectable a death as possible, for she wouldn't like to think of me going wailing and screaming to meet my Maker in front of the crowd that would be gathered outside in the yard. And I said that I'd do my best to compose myself and go with grace to meet Him.

'But it surely won't come to that – for it must be seen that a mistake's been made,' said Jane, a tone of yearning in her voice. 'A pardon will come for sure!'

My mother shook her head. 'We mustn't think on that, for who in the world would be trying to obtain a reprieve for us? No, 'tis only the gentry who can make representation to the law and get things changed.' She took my hand and held it tightly. 'We must prepare ourselves for the worst, Anne.'

'Although afterwards I intend to pursue the whoreson young master of that house and lay your death at his feet!' my father said with some anger. 'Yes, e'en if I have to go to Northumberland or whatever fartling place they've hid him.'

'Stay,' my mother said, 'for what good would that do?'

''Tis what a father *should* do!'

My mother sighed. 'So I'd be left without a husband as well as without a daughter, and then where would I be?'

'Tush!' went my father, muttering under his breath.

'Where are my brothers?' I asked after a moment.

'They'll be there in the yard,' said Ma, 'and more neighbours and friends from home as well.'

My heart felt like a stone. 'And all coming to see me die . . . ?'

'Not only for that,' Ma said soothingly, 'but to be with you at your last. To support and pray for you, and to help guide your soul to Paradise.'

I began weeping. 'My soul may not get there, for my body . . . my body will be cut into pieces!'

'Hush,' Ma said. 'I have spoken to the doctor, and he's promised to take the utmost care of your body and to treat it with respect. And . . . and . . .' But she turned away here with a sob, and couldn't continue.

'When you're brought home and put in the churchyard, I'll put flowers on your grave every day!' Jane said, and then she too burst out crying.

And so the minutes went on, and with each of them my mood changed: first fear and trembling, then bewilderment and disbelief, then sorrow, then railing against my fate and then a return to fear again. And by and by the cleric came in and spoke to my mother and father and knelt with them in prayer, and again addressed me, although of course I still would not admit guilt, for which he seemed very sorry.

Jane washed my face for me and brushed out my hair, and had brought a red ribband, which colour she said I must wear to show that I was brave, and with this we tied back my hair so that it would be out of the way of the hangman's noose and not get caught up. And the four of them kept asking how I was feeling, and if I would be strong, and each time I answered yes, although indeed I didn't feel well or strong, but just wanted the whole matter over with, for being dead could surely not be as bad as waiting to die and seeing your family suffer beside you.

I was worried about how they would be after, for my ma and pa looked very old and sad, and I tried to speak to Jane to tell her to mind them well and be a good daughter, but each time I got three words into the saying of this I'd break down and be unable to finish saying what I had started. During this time all of us were crying and shivering by turn, for the fire had gone out and it was a cold and dark grey morning, with sleet dripping from the sky, and it truly felt as if the end of the world was nigh.

I knew it was near my time when the prison governor came in with a sergeant-at-arms. Both spoke to me quite kindly and said that I had nothing to fear, I'd feel no pain and die quickly. And the soldier said that when I was pushed off the ladder, my father and brothers should hang on my legs if they had a mind to, for that would speed my end. The governor asked what were my worldly goods, and to whom did I wish to leave them, and I told him of all my clothes, including the bodice, and said that I wished to leave them to my mother to do with as she thought fit. He asked me to disrobe so that my clothes would not be spoiled, and I undressed down to my shift and gave my gown and cloak to Ma, although I was exceeding cold.

''Tis time to go,' the governor said, on hearing the clock strike. 'If you please, mistress . . .'

'Oh, give us just a little longer,' pleaded my ma, holding onto me tightly and looking at me with something like hunger in her expression.

He shook his head. 'We have two hangings today,' he said, 'and this is listed to be the first.'

'Then, by your leave, let our Anne be the second,' Pa begged. 'Allow us a little more time together.'

The governor shook his head. ''Twill be easier now, for the waiting is the worst part, and the crowd outside will have grown in an hour's time.' He regarded me with some sympathy. ''Tis more of an ordeal when it's a big crowd. More 'prentices to shout and throw rubbish.'

And so it was determined that I should go, and I kissed my family with a passion. My manacles were knocked off and the governor led me outside, telling me to put my hand on his shoulder to help support myself, for every part of me was trembling so violently I would otherwise have fallen. I was led along an open passageway and into the prison yard, which was bleak and desolate, with not so much as a blade of grass, a tuffet of green moss or a bird to be seen, but just ugly grey stone buildings running with rain and a strange and eerie feeling of anticipation in the air, as if the world was holding its breath.

The scaffold rose in front of me and, seeing the ugly reality of it, I swayed and almost fell, but the governor and sergeant caught me between them and held me upright. Standing beside this crude wooden structure, I looked around me and saw that the crowd consisted of perhaps eighty people. These included my brothers, some gowned scholars, learned men of the university, merchants, towns-people, the two carters who'd brought me in, the Reverend Coxeter, a governess from a dame school I once attended, several old neighbours and the squire from Steeple Barton, also a group of my fellow servants from Dun's Tew. Indeed it seemed very marvellous to me that almost everyone I'd ever known in my life was collected before me, and I was able to pick out each of their faces as if they were portraits in the gallery at the manor house. I saw a fair-haired young scholar with pity in his eyes, then my glance fell on Sir Thomas and I quickly turned away, for within his countenance I saw the hated face of Master Geoffrey.

As I turned from Sir Thomas my eyes alighted on John Taylor and for a brief moment my heart again leaped with joy, for his face was neither accusing nor vengeful but was filled with compassion and this gave me some small peace, for it told me that he'd forgiven me and that, at some pass-ing time, had even loved me. I smiled at him, though my head was swimming and I felt as if I was in a strange daydream, for 'twas the most curious thing to think that in a short moment I would cease to exist.

Beside the gibbet stood the hangman, wearing heavy clothes and a blanket against the weather, also a leather face mask so that he would not be recognized after. He was big and burly, looking very like the bogeyman that your ma tells you will come after you if you sin. And so he had.

'You must now kneel and make your peace with God,' said the cleric, and he bade me kneel down beside the scaffold. The Reverend Coxeter pushed his way through the crowd and knelt with me too, and close by were the scribes, holding their parchments under their capes to shield them from the rain and waiting to hear what I had to say. First the two clerical gentlemen and I sang a psalm together, which was number twenty-three and which I knew from long ago; then he asked me if I would confess my sins, for I had not much time now before I entered into Christ's Kingdom and came face to face with the Lord God.

This was a truly mighty thought and filled me with awe, and I could not but glance up to the solid grey sky and think about what He might be like and how I might be received by Him. I urged my mind upward while the rain pattered down on my face, but was offered no trace of the Heaven beyond.

'You must now confess all,' said the cleric.

'I will, and truly,' I answered up. 'I am guilty of the wicked sin of fornication.'

'Anything more?' he asked, urging me with his eyes to say what he wanted to hear.

I nodded. 'I am guilty of causing my family suffering.'

'And of what else?'

'Nothing of any consequence,' I said. I hesitated and then made brave to answer, 'And I would not be guilty of aught, except that I was led into sin in the house of my employer, Sir Thomas Reade.'

Alarm spread across the cleric's face at this and I wondered if his living came under the authority of Sir Thomas. He shook his head sorrowfully. 'Then may our Lord God forgive you all your sins and allow you to enter into the next world without shame,' he said, and offered me his hand to help me to my feet.

I began to tremble so frightfully that Ma ran forward and tried to put a blanket over my bare shoulders and embrace me again, but the hangman pushed her away, saying it would hinder things. She had a length of cord with her, which she requested should be tied around the bottom of my shift for modesty's sake, and he allowed her to do this. He gave me a hood, which he ordered me to put over my head, but my fingers were shaking so violently that they wouldn't do my bidding and the cleric had to fasten it for me. Just before he closed the flap that went across my eyes I looked across to my ma so that her dear face would be the last that I saw, and wanted to smile at her but could not, for I was sick with fear down to my very bones.

The hangman put a heavy coil of rope over me and around my neck, and bade me go up the ladder which stood beside the gibbet. I climbed seven steps, feeling it shaking beneath me, while the icy rain fell on my bare shoulders and trickled down the front of my shift. I braced myself for lewd shouts, or for rotten fruit to be thrown, but these did not come. I heard, though, a scream from Jane and some cries of protest from my family, and several other voices in the crowd shouting, 'Shame!' although I didn't know whether these meant shame on me for the crime I was accused of, or shame at my wretched fate.

I felt the hangman reach above my head and fix the rope that was to hang me and someone – I believe it was one of the scribes – called to ask if I had any last words.

'I protest my innocence,' I said, although my voice was so choked that I don't know if I was heard aright, 'and may God in his wisdom prove me innocent of the charges against me.'

'Anything else?'

'Only that all maidens who are tempted from the path

of virtue should think on me and be persuaded against such a course. And I pray that my death be quick and my family not suffer too much after.'

I began saying, 'And may God convey me swiftly—' but before I had scarce said the words '*to Paradise*' felt a violent push at my back and fell forward off the ladder. The noose around my neck tightened, and though I'd been told that – in order to make my passing all the quicker – I must try not to breathe, I found that this was impossible and, panicking, could not help but struggle to rasp in a minute amount of air through a throat now horribly constricted by the ring of rough rope. I'd wanted to make my last thoughts simple and wholesome, but there was no room for thoughts of any kind, for my senses were immediately assailed by a pain of such intensity that my head became filled with a searing white light.

I hung for a moment, suspended, felt my legs jerk and, unbidden, my body convulse, judder and twist in the air so that it seemed that I was flying twixt Heaven and Earth, then knew no more until I came into this drear darkness.

CHAPTER TWENTY-TWO

Robert, back in his lodgings, couldn't sleep. Scarlett, too, seemed fretful, and instead of perching quietly on the wooden railing that ran along the balcony abutting Robert's room, could be heard skittering up and down on the planks of its floor, pecking sharply at the occasional woodlouse that appeared from out of the sodden wood or a blade of grass that had grown through the knot-holes.

Thoughts of corpses floated through Robert's mind. Anne Green, and that other, dream-like one. His mother. To think that he'd recalled his mother when he hadn't known he'd ever seen her!

There were many answers to be sought to many questions, but his chief anxiety at that hour, that midnight hour when all ills and suspicions can seem overwhelming, was Anne Green. He somehow felt a responsibility for her well-being. Was Martha keeping watch over her? Would she call Mr Clarke if she felt her charge was in danger? How would a housemaid know such a thing? Suppose Anne just passed away in the night for want of warmth, a rousing cordial, or because her heart had faltered at a critical moment and had not been stimulated?

I want to see her.

Robert leaped out of bed. It wouldn't, he thought, hurt to check up on her. He'd find a way in to her for sure, for the apothecary's dwelling was one of a number of shops in the High Street which had interconnecting rooms, and all shared a back-yard privy.

On retiring the previous night, Robert had, in view of the extreme chill of his room and the lateness of the hour, gone to bed in all his clothes, so only had to don his hat and shoes to be ready. He took his heavy cloak from the hook on the door as he went out and, going across the balcony, threw Scarlett a scrap of hard bread.

Fifteen minutes later, treading quietly, or as quietly as possible on the creaking oak floorboards, Robert made his way along the corridor that led to Martha's room in Mr Clarke's house in the High Street. He hadn't been challenged on his way, for it was now near two o'clock in the morning and the whole of Oxford was asleep. Neither crier, night-soil man, whore nor late-night reveller had been encountered on his short journey.

A fierce snoring could be heard from Martha's room, and upon entering, Robert almost tripped over the recumbent body of Martha herself on the floor, wrapped around in what appeared to be a velvet curtain. He wasn't surprised at this: Martha obviously hadn't relished the thought of sleeping with such ghoulish company and had decided to leave the bed to Anne. This probably wouldn't have been discovered, for in the morning Martha would have been up and about before any of the doctors arrived, eager to claim her five shillings.

The fire in the room had been banked up in order to last until morning but was now only glowing, and Robert, stepping over Martha's form and lifting his candlestick so that the light would fall onto Anne's face, approached the bed with trepidation. Looking down at her still form, however, he noted with relief that her face held the same tranquil expression, as if she slept at peace. Placing the candlestick on the night table, he picked up one of her hands to count her pulse, then bent his ear to her mouth to note her breathing. When he straightened up he was smiling slightly to himself, for he thought her improved; her breathing was significantly deeper and her hands were less clenched than before. She seemed a little warmer, too, in spite of Martha's failure as a bedfellow.

'I thought you might have died,' Robert said to her in a low voice. 'I couldn't sleep, so I thought I'd come along and see how you fared.' As with Scarlett, he found himself speaking to her quite normally. Perhaps, he thought with something approaching levity, that was the answer: to try and see everyone as innocuous as a chicken or a cadaver. *They* weren't about to laugh at him or try to complete his sentences.

He brought a chair close to the bed and sat upon it, staring at Anne. It wouldn't hurt to talk to her, he thought. He'd been told once – by Dr Bathurst, if he remembered rightly – that hearing was the first and last faculty a human possessed, so perhaps speaking to her would somehow penetrate the lower levels of her consciousness. Besides, he found that he wanted to speak to her for his own sake; it would be a delight to address a pretty young woman and to know she wasn't going to stare at him as if he was a lunatic, or giggle behind her fingers.

'Are you going to live, Anne Green?' he asked and then, more reflectively, 'And where have you been while you haven't been living . . . when you haven't been *here*?' Boldly, he took up her hand and stroked it. 'You had many visitors yesterday. Scores of people came to stare. And today, later today, if you thrive, there'll be more. They sent horse to London last night to inform some very important doctors. They'll come. Indeed, Cromwell himself may come when he hears of these happenings.'

Anne drew in a slightly deeper breath, which caught in

her throat and made a soft growling sound. Robert felt her pulse; was her heart beating a little faster?

He paused and tucked a strand of hair behind her ear. 'I dare say, if you knew how many men had been staring at you, you'd ask for a mirror and brush and want to arrange your locks.' He glanced towards the sleeping form of Martha. 'Perhaps, tomorrow, Martha could be prevailed upon to help brush your hair. Or maybe wash your face, for 'tis still stained with tears from . . . from before, and they've poured several herbal preparations into your mouth, which have turned your lips and chin quite green.'

Anne Green slept on. Sleeping Beauty, Robert thought. Suppose she never woke? 'Yesterday, watching over you, I remembered something else. A part of my past and another cadaver. But not one that I have remembered before, for 'twas my mother.'

How odd, he thought, that he'd discovered such a thing after so many years. No wonder Dr Willis's chief goal was to try and discover the secrets of the brain, for it was surely a treasure house of miracles and marvels.

'I was but a child, you see, and they hadn't let me see her for days; they made excuses to prevent it. But the more they stopped me from seeing her, the more I yearned to do so. In the middle of the night, therefore, I rose and went to seek her.' He paused. 'But when I found her she was in a coffin, ready to be buried on the morrow. And then . . . then I can remember climbing onto the table, looking at her lying there in her nightdress and wanting to touch her . . .' He frowned, screwing up his face with the effort of trying to remember. 'And I *did* touch her – but don't recall what happened after.'

There was movement behind him. 'You were discovered with her body by one of the household, I should think,' came a voice, and Robert turned in alarm to see Dr Willis standing in the doorway, the shadow thrown by his candle shivering on the wall behind him. 'And then you were picked up and carried off to your nurse, and in the morning they told you it had all been nothing but a bad dream and you must forget about it.'

Robert got to his feet. 'F . . . f . . . f . . . for . . . g . . . give m . . .' he began.

Dr Willis raised a hand. 'Please,' he said. 'It's I who should ask your forgiveness for startling you. I decided to check on our patient and, hearing a voice, crept along here in order to discover what was afoot.'

'I . . . I . . . I . . .' Robert began.

'And strangely, found you speaking to her quite lucidly,' Dr Willis continued. 'Although, if I may be so bold, you normally have difficulty even saying your name, do you not?'

Robert nodded.

'This is a very curious phenomenon,' Dr Willis said thoughtfully. 'I myself have observed several children recently who, although stammering so badly that they could not be made sense of by others, were able to speak easily to their cat or dog.'

Robert smiled. 'Ch . . . ch . . . chicken!' he said, pointing at himself and then close to the ground at a chicken's height.

Dr Willis nodded. 'So,' he said, 'one day I may be able to investigate which part of the brain could cause such an anomaly. One day such mysteries may be revealed.' He stared at Anne. 'One day . . .'

Robert sat down again as Dr Willis put his candlestick on the windowsill, then positioned himself comfortably on the end of the bed. 'I struggle to understand certain disorders of the brain,' he confided; 'how some patients become terrified of cats or frogs for no particular reason, or feel compelled to carry out the same task over and over again. Why a man should of a sudden lapse into melancholy, or a woman fall to the ground in a fit and beat her hands upon the ground until they are bloody. All these seem to me to be disorders of the brain. And that may be to say, the soul.'

Robert stared at him, wishing he had his notebook.

'And as for our patient,' the doctor went on, indicating Anne Green, 'she may survive, but we must pray God that her soul is not lost.'

Robert looked at him questioningly.

'If she died, even for an instant, her spirit may have left her body and be unable to find its way back.'

Remembering what had been said at lectures, Robert looked at Dr Willis enquiringly and pointed to his head.

'Is the soul in the brain, you ask?' Dr Willis shrugged. 'I wonder sometimes if it's not either in the brain or the heart, but is fluttering around outside us. We don't know, cannot tell. My great fear is that this girl's soul has flown and will not come back . . . that if and when she awakes, she'll be but a spectre. A living form without a soul.'

Robert shook his head. Such a thought was unbearable and almost incomprehensible.

Dr Willis reached over and gripped his arm. 'But as to you,' he said, 'I heard what you were saying to our wench here, and have to tell you that I believe I know the cause of your impediment.'

Robert looked at him, startled.

'I believe that severe trauma in a child's life can cause it to develop a stammer. I don't begin to understand why, but sometimes a shock makes us internalize our feelings – we swallow them, in other words, and develop a reluctance to articulate anything. Do you know if you spoke normally at one time?'

Robert nodded, greatly intrigued.

'Perhaps, then, you began your wretched speech patterning after the shock of seeing your mother in her coffin.'

'P . . . per . . . per . . .' Robert began.

'And if you can now come to terms with what you saw all those years ago, perhaps discover the truth of it from your father, it may improve. It won't happen in a day, but . . .'

Robert's eyes gleamed with excitement. 'Th . . . th . . .' He took another breath. 'Th . . . th . . . thank you.'

Dr Willis smiled at him. 'So, to our charge here,' he said, indicating Anne. 'Shall we try and warm her a little more, seeing as Martha has proved less than reliable?'

Robert nodded. He wanted to say how elated he felt; how immensely grateful he was to Dr Willis for his advice; how he wouldn't rest now until his disability had been overcome. But of course he could not say any of that. Or not yet.

Robert, charged up by his memories and his enthusiasm over the task in hand, was still at Anne's bedside, awake and alert, as dawn broke the next morning. Dr Willis had gone home two hours before, leaving instructions for the patient's pulse to be taken regularly and, if anything untoward occurred, to wake Martha immediately and send her to him with a message. 'Keep talking to our patient, if you will,' he'd said to Robert, 'and, towards dawn, mix a little of the geneva in the flask with rainwater and try to get her to swallow it. One of us should be with you by eight o'clock.' He paused and a wry smile crossed his lips. 'If only to make sure that Sir Thomas Reade doesn't get in and endeavour to steal her away.'

By dawn, Robert had told Anne of every incident in his life and had hardly a thing left to say. He stood up, went to the window and stretched, trying – and failing – to make out the dark shape of the cart outside the gate. No streaks of light could yet be seen in the sky but, feeling that the morning was not far off, he decided to give Anne the cordial specified by Dr Willis. Accordingly, after rubbing her arms to stimulate and warm her blood, he prepared the drink, poured a little of it into a beaker and gently lifted up her head. At this point he remembered Dr Willis's fears about Anne lacking a soul and suffered a moment's alarm which made him falter. Such a thought was disturbing. What would someone without a soul be like? Dumb, dull and unresponsive? A foul fiend? A lunatic?

He forgot his fears as soon as he touched the beaker to Anne's mouth, however, for her lips parted slightly on contact. This had not happened any time before and was astonishing and significant. 'Here's something for you to drink,' he murmured, startled, 'and you may take more later, if you wish.' Her lips again moved and he stared at them, transfixed. 'Perhaps . . . perhaps you'd like a warming posset with butter and spices, or a chicken off the spit, or some syllabub,' he babbled. 'I dare say your fare in prison has been truly foul, for I hear tell that prisoners are reduced to eating week-old bread.'

His hand shaking slightly, he tipped a little more of the cordial into Anne's mouth and saw, to his excitement, that her throat moved with the swallowing reflex. This had not been encountered the previous day either.

''Twas well done, Anne!' he encouraged her. 'A little more?'

On these commonplace words her lids fluttered, then suddenly rose to reveal sea-blue eyes which fixed on Robert. He gasped aloud with shock and, staring at her with a mixture of alarm and delight, let her head fall back on the pillow and stepped back from the bed.

Anne's lips parted again and she whispered, her voice sounding faint, old and cracked, 'May God convey me swiftly to Paradise . . .'

PART TWO

CHAPTER TWENTY-THREE

I feel my eyelids flutter up and then my eyes move slowly around the room several times, as if they can't remember how to focus or where to direct themselves. After a short moment, however, they alight on a figure in the room sitting beside me, who, when I look with keener eye, turns out to be the fair-headed young fellow I'd briefly seen in the crowd at my hanging, close by to the gibbet, looking at me with great concern in his eyes. But why can I still see him? Am I still suspended, my head in the hangman's noose – or am I somehow viewing him from Heaven? And why is he staring at me, too, with something like awe and disbelief writ across his face?

My eyes move around to take in my surroundings and I discover that I'm in a small room with pale walls which are stained and blotched with damp in several places. The roof is sloping and there are shutters at the window, their green paint peeling to reveal the bare wood beneath. The stub of a candle burns on the windowsill and a faint light comes from outside, telling me 'tis either dawn or dusk. There's little in the way of furnishings apart from the bed I'm lying on, a nightstand, coffer and several hooks from which hang a few tousled clothes. To my mind it's a servant's room. But not the room in Dun's Tew which I share with Susan, nor any room I've been in before. If this is Heaven, I think, then 'tis passing strange that it should be so similar to Earth. Am I still to be a servant, then, in the nether-life? Should I not be an angel or a spirit creature?

When I think on this, something in my mind makes a connection. 'May God convey me swiftly to Paradise,' I try to say, but though my lips move I hardly make a sound, for my throat feels thick and parched.

The youth beside me gasps. He takes my hand, seemingly to comfort me. 'I . . . I . . . it . . . it's . . .' he begins, and then he stops and takes a deep breath. He tries to speak again, fails, then pounds his fist into his palm as if he's angry with himself. He sits for another moment staring at me with disbelief, as if I might vanish like a street-huckster's monkey, and then stands up and takes three steps across the floor. He immediately retraces these and sits down again, shaking his head. 'C . . . c . . . can't,' he mutters. 'Can't go.'

I wonder if he's mad, or if he's part of Heaven or Hell. Or – I have a sudden new thought – maybe I'm not in either of those places, a last-minute reprieve having arrived and prevented my hanging. No, that cannot be, for I can remember my last moments: Ma's face, the scream from Jane, my final words and the hard thump on my back as I was pushed off the ladder. Am I in limbo? Is limbo, then, a servant's bedroom?

My head begins to swim as if I've imbibed too much ale. 'May God convey me swiftly to Paradise,' I mouth again, for this seems like a charm against the darkness and, besides, is all I can think of to say.

There is a sudden scream from someone lying on the floor of the bedroom, and when I look down there's a girl there, all wrapped round in fabric. Her hair is tousled and frizzy, her face puffy from sleep. 'She's alive!' she screams. 'The corpse speaks!' Still wrapped up, she moves on her backside towards the door as if she wants to get as far away from us as she can. 'Oh Lord, she spoke!'

I look at her in some surprise, thinking that if anyone should be frightened, it should be I, waking from a night-fright in this unfamiliar place amongst strangers and all unknowing about how I came to be here.

'I . . . it . . . it . . .' the youth begins, and he is talking to her now.

She darts a look at him. 'I stayed with her some of the night, sir!' she says. '*Most* of it, I should say – till just before you came in. I went on the floor to give her more room.

Oh, you won't tell the other gents, will you?'

He shakes his head.

'Shall I go for Mr Clarke?' she asks, not taking her eyes off me as she unwraps herself.

He nods and makes some strange forward looping movements with his hands.

'And the other doctors?' she asks.

He nods emphatically and vigorously, as much as to say that yes, everyone must come, and she disappears harum-scarum down the corridor.

He stares back at me, draws a breath, closes his eyes an instant. 'D . . . d . . . don't . . . don't . . . be frightened,' he says, and he takes my hand in his. ''Twill . . . b . . . be . . . all right.' There is another pause and after a further deep breath he goes on, 'Y . . . you . . . you . . .' He speaks carefully, pointing to me as he says the word. '*You* h . . . h . . . have been saved.'

I consider this. I *have been saved*. But from what, exactly? You can't be saved from Heaven, so it must be that I've been saved from Hell.

'You did not die,' he says, and then frowns and repeats, 'You did not die. Or . . . or perhaps you did. B . . . but now, certainly, you are not dead.'

What am I, then? I ask silently.

'You . . . you are still in the world of the living. D . . . d

. . . do you understand?'

I continue to stare at him and discover I am shivering all over with cold. I look down at myself and find that I'm wrapped in a coarse blanket, and looking underneath this, discover a horrid and soiled undersmock. No, I think, I do *not* understand. I remember the long dream I'd had where I'd been alive but trapped in the ghastly darkness of my grave. What had come of that?

As I lie staring at him, my mind a perfect turmoil of wondering, he takes off his cloak and tucks it round me. I am suddenly conscious of an overwhelming thirst but, strangely, can't think of the right words to ask for what I want. I open my mouth and point inside, and then, feeling exhausted with the effort of that, my lids flutter down. Every part of me aches, I realize. My limbs, my breasts, my belly, my back – my throat and neck most of all.

'Y . . . you . . . you're thirsty,' he says. 'You want water? Some beer? Milk?'

I open my eyes and nod to any of these and he gets up, and then sits down again. 'I . . . I can't leave yet,' he says. 'Your grasp on life is too tenuous. W . . . will you take a little more of this geneva?' I shake my head, for the spirit is coarse and fiery and what I long for is something soothing and warm.

'The doctors will be here soon, and then I'll go and mix

you something else. S . . . something hot against the day, perhaps.' He opens the window shutter a little wider and a morning light falls into the room. ''Tis snowing again, and monstrous cold.' He smiles at me. 'B . . . but I should tell you that my name is Robert Matthews and I am a scholar of New College, Oxford. And I . . . I'm very pleased to make your acquaintance, Anne Green.'

I want to smile a little, for he sounds so strange and formal, and besides, a gentleman of his standing is out of place in a servant's room.

'W . . . we are in Oxford at the house of Mr Clarke the apothecary,' he says. He glances outside. 'Your mother,' he begins, and I feel a jolt of shock that he should speak of my ma. 'Your mother and others of your family, I believe, are waiting just a little way off.'

I close my eyes again and feel tears seep from under my lids, for although I can't say what has happened to me, I do know that I long to see my ma.

'As soon as the doctors arrive, we'll send message to your family to let them know that you live.'

I live! I think, and wriggle my fingers and open and close my eyes several times, just to ensure that I can. Just to prove to myself that I am not under the ground.

How strange it all is. My head swims and I struggle to understand. Did it all happen? Did the gaol and the trial and the hanging really occur, or have I imagined the whole episode in a dream? I put my hand up to my neck and fit the open span of my fingers around it. No, I believe it really happened, for I can feel bruising there, and some swelling and pain. I move my fingers higher and feel the sore patch on my face, which seems grazed with blood.

'All . . . all the damage to your face comes from where the rope bruised you,' Robert says. 'I . . . is it sore? When Mr Clarke comes he'll let us have some wintergreen.'

I nod, satisfied, and, feeling myself drifting towards sleep, strain to stay awake, for if I sleep then I might return to that dark and drear place I was in before; that mysterious place where the shadow of death lingered.

I feel Robert's fingers at my neck, pressing gently. After a moment he says, 'Your pulse is regular and strong. Dr Willis will be very pleased with you; as will the others.'

He says something more, and his words fade and fall into my head, drifting along like twigs in a brook as sleep advances and retreats by turn.

In spite of my endeavours, I believe that I sleep for a while, for when I open my eyes the light in the room is pinker. I hear voices, and two gowned gentlemen come into the room side by side, both looking towards me eagerly. I want to get up and curtsey to them, but I know that I would fall down in a heap if I tried to do such a thing, for I have scarce the strength to open and close my eyes, let alone bend my legs in obeisance.

'Is this true?' one of them asks as he enters the room.

'She has opened her eyes? Spoken?' asks the other.

'Sh . . . sh . . . she . . .' Robert begins several times, and then sighs impatiently.

''Tis no matter,' the first says to him, very kindly. He approaches the bed and takes up my wrist. 'Now, don't be afeared, my dear,' he says to me. 'I'm Doctor Willis and I'm just going to count your heartbeats.'

'We can see from her colour alone how she's improved!' says the other, who is a handsome man and strong of feature. He peers at me and smiles. 'I'm Doctor Petty. Now, don't be frightened. You're doing very well.'

Dr Willis counts under his breath, looking at the watch he holds in his other hand. 'Excellent!' he says. He puts his hand into mine. 'Now, my dear young lady,' he asks, 'can you wriggle your toes and squeeze my fingers?'

Obediently, I do both these things – and I can't help smiling as I do them, for he looks so very amazed as he watches me.

'Merciful Lord!' he says, and of a sudden he slips down onto his knees beside the bed, his hands folded together and his head bowed. I'm surprised at this, for I'd thought him to be a physician and not a cleric – but perhaps he's both. 'Our prayers have been answered,' he says. 'Thank you, Lord, for sparing her life and for allowing us, your servants, to act through you. And thank you for restoring her soul to her.'

Conscious that he is praying for me, I think it meet to whisper, 'And may God convey me swiftly to Paradise.'

They smile and look at each other. 'Those were her last words!' Dr Willis says.

'A . . . and her f . . . f . . . first,' adds Robert.

'But we don't want that now,' says Dr Petty to me. 'We rather hope that God does *not* convey you swiftly to Paradise, my dear, for if He does, He will undo all the good we've done.'

Dr Willis gets up from his knees in such a hurry that he stands on his gown and tears it. That will be a difficult tear for a servant to repair, I think, for the fabric's old and the threads are pulled. 'William, William!' he says. 'This is a great day. A miraculous day. A day when we have witnessed His divine intervention with our own eyes.'

Dr Petty nods thoughtfully. 'Yes,' he says. 'Or . . .' He looks at the other with one eyebrow raised. 'Or perhaps the hangman's noose had a faulty knot and didn't press where it should have done to despatch its victim.'

Dr Willis gives no indication of having heard this.

'Today the bells of Heaven will ring out in joy!'

'And the bells of Christ Church, if I have anything to do with it,' adds Dr Petty.

The girl who had been sleeping on the floor of the room – I hear her named as Martha – raddles out the grate and lays and lights a fire, and another man comes in carrying a bleeding bowl and some cloths. He is introduced to me as Mr Clarke, the apothecary whose house we are in. Next to arrive is a tall man with two assistants; he is Dr Bathurst. All stand round and gaze at me, marvelling and exclaiming by turn. Robert is sent down to the herb garden to see if there's any wintergreen growing fresh, but it's not the season, so he comes back with dried leaves from the shop, which are quickly made into a balm and applied to my throat and neck. Mr Clarke goes to get the best honey from his lavender bees and Martha is told to add three spoonfuls of this to some warm milk. She and Robert then lift my head gently so that I can drink it, and it soothes my throat most excellently.

Two more gentlemen arrive who are said to be masters at the university. They are told of my progress, my heart-beat and my breathing and they join the little group around my bed. Martha is instructed to go to the baker's for a fresh loaf of white bread and then crumb the inside of this and sop it into warm milk for me. I need nourishment, they say, for I have been through a great ordeal.

'To Heaven and back!' says one of the masters.

'I'll go when I can find the time,' Martha says, and Mr Clarke looks at her most severely, telling her that the day will be a busy one and she must be prepared to work hard. She whispers something in his ear and he nods, then solicits some coins from the two doctors and presses these into her hand.

I'm bled into a bowl, my forehead is soothed with oils, and one or other of the men there takes my pulse, looks into my mouth or just stands and stares at me. I marvel greatly at my circumstances; at how one moment I can be in the meanest gaol amongst rogues and vagabonds with not a friend in the world, and the next be treated with as much deference as a queen.

'Is there anything you want?' Dr Petty asks, his words drifting into my thoughts. 'Or is any part of you in pain?'

With my fingers I point to my tongue, for it feels strange and is numb at the tip. I frown a little; I can think the words I want to say, but not speak them. This must, I think, be a little like the trouble that afflicts Robert.

Three men look into my mouth and examine the part of my tongue I'm pointing to.

'It's been bitten,' one says.

'But is not furry . . .'

'I think you must have chewed on it when you were hanging,' says the third.

The apothecary looks in my mouth also. 'And to treat it . . . perhaps a salve made from the green fruit of the blackberry? 'Tis more usually employed for ulcers in the mouth, but 'twill do, I think.'

The others nod agreement. Robert is sent down to the shop to choose the ingredients and returns to say the assistant has them and will compound them into a paste.

My mind is set on what Robert promised earlier, and when he comes close I signal to him and point outside. He knows what I mean.

'H . . . h . . . her f . . . f . . . family,' he says to the others.

'Of course!' says Dr Willis.

'At this moment!' cries Dr Petty, and they decide between themselves that he, Dr Willis and Robert will go to tell them that I'm alive. On the way out Dr Petty speaks to Martha, who is bent over the fire and looking agitated, her hair still frowsy. She nods but sighs when he's gone and looks at me rather crossly.

In a moment or two she brings up a bowl of warm water from downstairs and, asking the other gentlemen if they'll kindly wait outside for a moment, produces a chamber pot from under the bed. Ascertaining that I don't want to use this, she replaces it and then takes a muslin cloth, dampens it in the bowl of water and, rubbing a morsel of soap on this, wipes me all over, being very gentle around my sore face and neck. She removes the bedraggled red ribband, brushes my hair, and brings out a pink ribband to tie back my tresses. Finally she goes to the coffer and gets out a worn cotton nightdress, which she changes for the stained undersmock I'm wearing. I can't think of what to say or how to thank her for all these ministrations, so merely smile at her gratefully and squeeze her hand.

She seems to unbend a little and smiles at me. 'You look better now,' she nods. 'Indeed, for a dead corpse you look a great deal alive.'

I return the smile. *A dead corpse*, I think. I close my eyes for a moment to wonder about all the things that are happening, and why they are doing so. And when my mind clears a little, I reach some kind of an understanding and believe I know the truth of it. And the truth is this: *I was hanged, but did not die.*

CHAPTER TWENTY-FOUR

I may have slept again for a moment after that, for when I wake I feel more certain about what's happening and more accepting of it – although I still cannot understand such a thing. I look anxiously for my family, but they do not appear and I'm in a fright of concern about them, for they'll surely never believe what has happened. Besides, my pa is not used to conversing with gentlemen and may have taken himself off in a fright on their approach.

Three more men from the university come into the room to look me over. Two of these fall to their knees and pray by my bedside to give thanks to God for my deliverance and, unsure of how to compose myself but knowing I must show a serious countenance, I close my eyes while they are doing this and press my hands together into an attitude of prayer. 'May God convey me swiftly to Paradise . . .' I whisper, and they smile at me and look wondering.

Martha complains about her bedroom being hardly big enough for such goings-on, and it's decided that I should be moved to Mr Clarke's room. Accordingly, a witty and waggish fellow, one who came in with Mr Bathurst, picks me up bodily, bedstuffs and all, and takes me to Mr Clarke's own bedroom further down the corridor. Here I am queen indeed, for I'm placed in a proper wooden tester, with gold and magenta hangings at the head and a deep feather mattress. The room is panelled, a quilted silk carpet sits on the floor, and there are paintings on the walls: two large ones depicting highland beasts, and smaller paintings of herbs and flowers. I've not been in such a room before – or only to clean – and feel anxious about it, for I have put Mr Clarke out of his own bed. He, however, seems extreme happy to have me there and says to the others, 'I am a made man. We are all made men!' – by which I understand that they'll receive recognition for what has occurred.

One other thing goes with me into Mr Clarke's room: the coffin which they tell me I was placed in after my hanging. This is propped up by the window with its lid standing beside it, and gives me the horrors whenever I look upon it.

Robert and the others are away a long time and I begin to wonder if my parents might have gone home. I find out later, however, that the doctors had difficulty in making them understand what had happened, for my pa refused to believe it at first, thinking that they had come from Sir Thomas and were playing some cruel trick on them.

Martha brings a bowl of bread and milk and I eat it in little mouthfuls, for it pains my throat to swallow. At last I hear noises: lots of footsteps in the hall and the voices of the two doctors floating out loud and cheerful as they shepherd everyone up the stairs, and I become very excited.

'In here now! In here!' Mr Clarke calls, and in they troop: the doctors first, and then Ma, Pa, Jane and my two brothers, all silent, awkward and awestruck, which I know is because none of them has been a visitor to such a house before.

I smile, but don't know what to say to them; for that one single Godly sentence I have in my head is not altogether appropriate.

'Well!' Ma says, staring at me with her hand pressed to her mouth. 'Well!'

Jane takes two steps into the room, looks around at the furnishings and her jaw drops. Pa and my brothers whip off their old felt hats and stand awkwardly, bowing around at the gentlemen gathered there. Jane sees what they're doing and begins curtseying and, strangely, gives a curtsey to me as well.

This makes me laugh and she laughs too, and this makes things easier.

I struggle to sit up and hold out my arms to Ma but find

myself weak as a kitten and fall back on the pillows. Ma comes to me then, and holds me, and we weep for a considerable time. After this I kiss everyone, then Ma and Jane take up positions by my bed while Pa and my brothers go out into the hall in order to leave more space for the gentry.

Finding that I'm still unable to speak, the doctors apply a plaister to my throat, which warms it greatly, and after I've eaten a second bowl of bread and milk I find myself able to say a few words, but croakily. I say *Thank you*, first, and *Hello* to some visitors, and then I say the names of all my family, which pleases them enormously, and 'tis like when an infant babbles for the first time. It pleases the doctors, too, for Robert tells me later that some of them feared for my sanity until they heard me begin to speak. After this the words arrive all the time. I do not speak to anyone to ask what I long to, however, which is for news of John Taylor. Has he heard that I've survived? Does he care enough to visit me and accept my apologies?

Two youths arrive who are scholars with Robert. 'Ah,' says Dr Petty cheerily (and indeed everyone is very cheerful). 'Here come a couple of fellows who are the very flowers of the nobility and gentry of the kingdom!'

The scholars bow around them, and Ma and Jane curtsey once more.

'Congratulations on your new-born patient!' they say, greeting Robert with a punch to the arm.

'G . . . good morning,' he says to them, and they all hoot and ask him whether he's in his cups that he can speak so well.

He says, 'No, not at all,' very carefully, and then grins, delighted.

They both then gather round and gape at me as if I'm a sideshow at the May Fair.

'We saw you yesterday in your shift, madam!' one says, winking at me. He is fine and dandy, with long, curling hair and a ruffle of lace at his throat. When Martha comes in he winks at her also and makes her blush, which makes me long to tell her not to believe any such sweet-talk from him, for he's a master and she a servant, and I know from my own experience that any coupling would not prove a happy one.

Another of the scholars wants to make a drawing of me and retires to one side of the bed with a block of paper. 'I made two when I thought you were dead and this will complete the set,' he says.

More and more people arrive, and the one who was drawing me has his position taken by an elderly gentleman who brings his own shooting stick to sit upon. A hackney carriage comes from Cambridge containing some medical men, and they say there may be some from London on the morrow.

'And all to see you,' Dr Petty says.

'And this is just the start of it,' says Dr Willis.

The new medical men stand at the end of my bed, stare at me and marvel, and then look at my coffin and say that such a thing has never happened before and that I was indeed fortunate to have been *nearly* dissected by such learned men, for others might not have been able to revive me.

I hear Dr Willis say, 'Of course, we have no idea when the light of life goes out and the soul departs . . .'

'Or when the quick become dead,' adds Dr Petty, and there is general agreement in the room that this is true.

The two scholars go off to the coffee house and are quickly replaced by double that number. Shortly after this a messenger brings word that two great ladies have come all the way from Windsor and wish to set eyes on me.

This causes quite a little stir in the room. I have my hair combed out once more (Jane makes an effort to curl it) and a walkway is made through the people so that these two ladies – Dr Willis says that both are countesses – may approach me whilst everyone else stays at a respectful distance. The room goes silent as they arrive and so do I, for I can scarce believe that I am the purpose of their visit. They are finely dressed in velvet gowns, one in maroon and one in dark green, with fur-trimmed cloaks over, and when they throw their hoods back their hair is dressed in ringlets with pearls threaded through. Ma sinks into a deep curtsey, but Jane has forgotten to do so and I see her out of the corner of my eye, her jaw hanging loose in wonder.

'Is it really true, my dear?' the maroon gown asks. 'Were you hanged yesterday?'

I nod, feeling shy.

'And what was it like before you were awoken by the doctors? Can you remember where you were?'

I shake my head and their faces fall.

'Nothing?' they ask. 'You can't remember a thing?'

'I . . . I was just in darkness,' I answer.

'But surely you must have seen *something*,' the green gown asks, and she pouts her lips a little.

'Was it something very private and personal?' says the other.

'For we are simply agog to know!'

The green lowers her voice. 'Someone we know who suffered a fit and nearly died said she'd seen a vision of Paradise, and it was all hot sun, green pastures and silver rivers, as beautiful as could be . . .'

I nod slowly, wondering if I could have seen such things and forgotten about them after.

'Angels!' says the maroon. 'Some people on point of death say that they've seen angels with flowing white wings and silver harps.'

I nod more eagerly. 'I believe I did see some angels,' I say, remembering the blurry shapes that had passed across my vision in the darkness. 'Four of them, walking together.'

Their eyes light up. 'I knew it!' green gown says.

'She may be a prophetess!'

I don't know what this is, but I nod, and before I can help myself am agreeing with them that I'd seen all sorts of things: strange wild beasts walking with lambs, rivers of silver, flying cherubs and all manner of heavenly creatures together in a glorious garden in which was growing an abundance of sweet-smelling flowers.

When the ladies leave, much pleased with me, Dr Petty and Dr Willis clear the room for a short while, saying that I need some rest. Everyone goes out, even Ma and Jane, then Dr Petty sits on the bed and takes my hand. 'Now, Anne,' he says, 'I want you to tell me exactly what you saw when you were in that other place – before you awoke and found yourself in Martha's bedroom.'

I feel myself blush.

'And you must tell us the truth, mind,' says Dr Willis, speaking very seriously and kindly.

I lie back on my pillows. 'I think I *did* see angels.'

'What were they like?' Dr Willis asks.

'They were somewhat blurred,' I say. 'But seemed very much like angels.'

Dr Petty gives me a reproachful look. 'Anne . . . ?'

I look away.

'And what of the strange wild beasts and the cherubs?' asks Dr Willis.

My head drops. 'Perhaps I didn't see them. But I thought . . . thought that was what the ladies wished to hear.'

'Oh, they did, certainly,' says Dr Willis.

'But you mustn't be tempted to say such things,' Dr Petty says, 'for on such a flimsy basis, whole religions can be formed. Some would need no more excuse to put you at the head of the Church like Mother Mary, and a web of mummery and superstition formed about you.'

Dr Willis looks as if he regrets there not being any angels or silver streams. 'The shapes you saw were probably those forms we all see under our closed eyelids,' he says with a sigh.

The next visitors who arrive – two elderly and very learned gentlemen from Cambridge, in plush coats and plumed hats – I am more reticent with. I hardly say a word (for anyway, my throat is paining me), but Jane chatters like a jackdaw, smiling as she recounts the family's joy and weeping copiously as she tells of our previous sufferings. The gentlemen are most sympathetic and, as they get up to leave, give me a gold angel. It must be used, they say, to purchase whatever is necessary for my complete recovery.

This is treasure indeed, for 'tis worth ten whole shillings. The family come round the bed to marvel at the very goldness of the coin, and Jane bites it to make sure 'tis not counterfeit.

I find that I am more at ease in the grand bed now. I know that I have *not*, but I begin to feel that I've done something particular and special to be so lauded. Only two things prevent me from being truly happy: firstly, I fear that Sir Thomas may arrive at any time and take me to be hanged again; secondly, there is someone that I long to see and beg forgiveness from.

There are more arrivals. Dr Willis brings a fellow to me. 'This man is from Mr Burdet the printer and he is to write up a pamphlet about you,' he says, 'so you must tell him truthfully whatever you can remember. And no more!' he adds.

I nod and the fellow brings a chair and sits down beside the bed. People jostle all around him so he asks Jane to hold his bottle of ink, then takes out a quill and a block of paper. ''Twill make an excellent good story,' he says to me. 'An *improving* story wherein people may learn that good can triumph, and that justice may be found on Earth as well as in Paradise.'

'And what will it be called?' Jane asks him.

'*Newes from the Dead*,' he says. 'For your sister here was dead and now is not. And she brings us news from that other world.'

I look towards the doctors with some unease.

'We'll start with the angels,' says the scribe. 'The Countess of Wimborne says that you saw angels . . .'

Embarrassed, I shake my head.

''Twas all a misunderstanding,' says Dr Petty.

The fellow frowns, rather disappointed. 'Let me have your prayers, then, Mistress Green, for I must record your own words to the Lord. 'Tis said that when you awoke here, you began speaking at exactly the point where you left off on the gibbet.'

I glance towards Robert, who is nodding at me. 'When I awoke I found myself saying, "May God convey me swiftly to Paradise . . ."'

'Which were indeed her last words as she was hanged,' says Dr Petty.

Dr Willis approaches the bed. 'It was as if Mistress

Green were a clock whose weights had been taken off a while, and afterward hung on again.'

'Wise words, sir,' says the scribe, and he writes them down. He asks me how often I attend church and I am about to reply when there is a stir outside in the corridor and a little 'prentice boy runs in, pushing through the people. He works at a carpenter's, I think, for he wears a dusty brown apron down to the ground and pale sawdust frosts his hair and eyebrows.

'Whatever is it?' Dr Willis asks.

'Please, sir,' puffs the 'prentice, 'Mr Parker said I should come and tell you the news. He just heard from the Reade house, see. Got 'structions to go there straight.'

'Who has? What do you mean, boy?' asks Dr Petty.

'Mr Parker,' said the boy, panting some, 'says I must tell you he has been instructed to go over to Dun's Tew and measure for a coffin. A coffin for Sir Thomas Reade, who has upped and died!'

'Sir Thomas? *Dead?*' enquires Dr Willis in a shocked voice.

There is a moment's silence and someone calls, 'Oh, behold God's providence!' and several men fall to their knees and begin praying aloud. As for me, I'd long wished him dead and at first wonder, with some guilt, if my wishes have worked a curse on him (but this guilt does not last long).

The scribe looks shocked for a moment, then I hear him murmur, 'Excellent . . . excellent,' before the nib of his pen begins scratching along the pad again. 'Behold God's providence . . .' I hear him mutter under his breath.

CHAPTER TWENTY-FIVE

I have slept well, or so the physicians who surround me declare, and my voice is sounder, the swelling and bruising to my neck much improved and my heartbeat strong. I have even managed to stand for just a moment, before being overcome with a fit of dizziness. My brothers have had to return to their workplace but Jane, Ma and Pa are close by, and last night Jane and Ma shared my bed with me.

I feel leaden in my body, but my mind whirls away like a snowflake and there are notions and images running through my head, as many, varied and entwined as ribbands on a maypole. Why have I been saved? What is meant by such an occurrence? Can it be true – as I was told by one gentleman visitor – that God means to begin a new religious order through me? I sincerely hope it is not, for I don't feel able to lead such an order, to seek followers or e'en know how I would address them.

I think about Sir Thomas's death and (although I own it wicked of me) feel mighty content about it, being unable to spare a thought for his grieving widow or his surviving family. How selfish a person I have become – but how very strange it is that he should die while I should live!

The scholars are about my bed early and half fill the room, for their masters have set them a task to write a poem about my situation and there is much laughter as they try out their lines (although some I cannot understand a word of, being written in a language they say is Latin). Master Wren's produces laughter, for no one can tell what it means, and Dr Petty says to him, 'By the Lord, Christopher, you had better look to your other talents rather than poesy.'

By the time the clock strikes ten o'clock the scholars half fill the room, and they are shooed out by Dr Willis to attend lectures. Robert puts down his papers – as well as writing the poem, he has been recording my treatments – comes to me and presses my hand. 'I . . . I . . . I fear you will have a tiring day,' he says, 'for it seems that the whole w . . . world are on their way to see you.'

''Tis of no matter,' I say, for I am enjoying my reign as queen. I do not even have to speak much, but merely lie in the feather bed and smile graciously as people kiss my hand. I think 'tis the best and easiest employment I have ever had.

I thank Robert again for his ministrations and some

moments later the first of that day's proper visitors arrive: a group of clerical gentlemen who wish to pray at my bedside. They are joined by a deputation of apothecaries, a gentleman I am told is Cromwell's deputy in Oxford, and a party of scientific men who have just arrived on the coach from London and have not e'en stopped at the tavern for refreshment. After these, a finely dressed lady arrives with two maids accompanying her, her gown tricked out with so many petticoats that it takes up the space of six men. While she is still laying her hands on me and mouthing softly, 'Oh, my dear, how you have suffered . . .' a swarthy woman and her daughter come in and scare her away. It appears that they are fairground people, and they ask if they can buy my nightdress to cut into squares and sell as lucky charms.

I think this an excellent idea and apply to Dr Petty for permission, but he refuses.

'We will not have people making money out of such gewgaws,' he says.

'Isn't that rather hard, William?' Mr Clarke says.

'Maybe. But such things are hocum-pocum nonsense and have no place in the practice of medicine,' says Dr Petty. 'They are just in it to make money.'

'But will we not make money from what we have achieved with the girl?'

'No, we will not,' says Dr Petty in a low voice. 'We will make more: we will make our reputations.'

Martha is busying herself and has heard some of this conversation. 'Anyway,' she says, ''tis *my* old nightdress and not lucky at all.'

This matter with the fairground women has given Dr Willis an idea, however. The doctors speak together and, the room being full to bursting again, it is cleared of all visitors, Dr Willis saying that this is so that I may take sustenance and have certain medical observations made.

When just my family are left, Dr Willis explains that as news of me spreads further afield, the number of people coming to see me will increase. 'And I fear we may not be able to admit them all to see Anne, for this house just cannot contain them,' he says.

'Do you want her to come home now, then?' Ma asks, somewhat faintly, and I know she is envisaging a parade of finely dressed gentry treading the path to our little cottage.

Dr Willis shakes his head. 'She must stay with us for a few more days yet – perhaps a week – until we are sure of her complete recovery. But to help us all, we intend to restrict those coming to see her by charging them a fee.'

'Like a show at the May Fair?' Jane asks.

'No, young mistress, like a proper scientific display,

such as the universities put on from time to time.'

'The poorer sort will thus stay away, but the quality will not be refused,' says Dr Petty.

'We will charge one shilling,' said Dr Willis, 'and in a short time – mark my words – we will have enough to pay for all the medicines used on Anne, for our attendance at her bedside and for the legal fees that will be needed to obtain her a full pardon.'

'And what's left after will go some way towards her marriage portion,' said Dr Bathurst kindly, 'for every girl should have a dowry of some kind.'

My family say nothing to this last, but I know that they are wondering who ever would take me.

The day proceeds with my father standing at the door holding a wooden box Mr Clarke has obtained and rattling this as people walk up the passage. They place their shillings in this without question (some give more) for a sign has been put downstairs in the shop warning of the charge, and those unwilling to pay do not venture the stairs.

I am surprised at how quickly Pa falls into his role; 'Come see Anne Green, the miracle woman!' he calls like a mountebank. 'The woman that was hanged and lived to tell the tale! Come and see proof of God's mighty providence!' And sometimes, if the people are very grand, Jane goes over to greet them the doorway, brings them to my bedside and affects an introduction with much flim-flam and curtseying.

Dinner is at noon, and straight after this I receive a further small deputation of gentlemen from London, who speak at long and boring length to Dr Willis and Dr Petty, then come and stand at the foot of my bed and shake their heads at me. I try to be alert so that they may see that I'm fully recovered, but my eyelids are beginning to droop with tiredness when I hear a discussion at the bedroom door and a voice pleading to be let in to see me without payment.

A male voice says, 'For on hearing the news I threw off my apron, jumped on the horse I was shoeing and rode here without a pause.'

'I'm sorry, sir,' I hear my pa say. ''Tis a shilling for all and sundry.'

'But I did not think to put money in my pocket, man!' the voice says urgently. 'Do let me pass!'

Fully awake once more, I stare over the heads of the medical gentlemen and can just see the top of a battered felt hat.

'I'll bring a shilling to you directly! Just let me see her now.'

'I'm sorry, sir, but I'm going to have to turn you away,' my father says, then adds jovially, 'Indeed, I would lose my job if I let you in without payment.'

I hear a soft swear word and a sigh of exasperation, then comes the rustle of gowns and the clack of leather shoes as more visitors come down the corridor. There is a clink as their money goes in the box.

Jane is sitting cross-legged on the bed sewing some gloves. 'Who was that who spoke then – the man without a shilling?' I ask her with some urgency. 'Go quickly and see!'

She nods at me but doesn't move fast enough for my liking, so that I have to ask the medical men to kindly shift to one side to enable me to see round them and to the doorway.

But there is no one there now but three Puritan women looking like crows in their black moiré gowns.

'Go after that man!' I say to Jane, and I push her off the bed. 'Quickly!'

She goes. But doesn't have to go far, because the man in question has heard my voice, turned back and now waits in the doorway.

He takes off his hat and stands awkwardly, staring at me. He's still in his working clothes with a soot-streaked face, grimy arms and hair caught back in a band. He has not, today, scrubbed his hands or cleaned his fingernails.

I call, 'Let him in, Pa!' and John Taylor comes toward me slowly.

We stare at each other. There's much to say, but that

cannot be started yet. Instead I say softly, 'Fie, John Taylor, am I not even worth a shilling?'

'Nay,' he answers, 'but you are worth silver and gold to me.'

And I look at him and know that my life story can begin again, as if I am newly born, and count myself as both the most cursed woman, and the most fortunate, that ever was on this Earth.

Author's Notes

I first came across the story of Anne Green in 2004 while listening to a programme on BBC's Radio Four. A panel was discussing the way in which women throughout the ages have been prosecuted for infanticide – the murder of a baby – when they had actually suffered a stillbirth or (if the child had lived a short while) a cot death. Anne's case was mentioned, the story told of how she was hanged for infanticide and subsequently revived, and I was gripped. Her death and revival have been documented many times over the years from the point of view of the doctors who were instrumental in her revival, but I wanted to write the story from Anne's perspective. Naturally, therefore, although the main thrust of the story is absolutely true, all the conversations and trivia are from my imagination.

Anne was a serving maid in the house of Sir Thomas Reade in 1650 and thus could have been present when Charles I visited the house to say his last goodbyes to Queen Henrietta some years previous to this. The present owners of the manor house in Dun's Tew kindly allowed me access to the buildings and grounds, and although these have been much altered over the years, the huge dovecote still remains. There was also a trace of the old outside privies for the servants, presumably still in the same place as the ones which had existed in Anne's day.

Sir Thomas's heir, Geoffrey Reade, was sixteen or seventeen at the time of Anne's hanging, but was spirited out of the county before her trial and was not heard of again. Sir Thomas's displeasure at his grandson's actions was, perhaps, illustrated by the fact that under the terms of his Will, Geoffrey Reade only received a farm in Northampton, when he might have been expected to receive considerably more of the lands and great manors owned by the family. Sir Thomas was said to have been present at Anne's dissection, but was taken ill and died one or two days after her revival, which was taken as further proof of Anne's innocence and God's judgement.

Anne, following the stillbirth, was described as miserably ill and weak, and the conditions in Oxford Gaol were said to be 'indescribable . . . with lack of sanitation, warmth and lighting'. She would have had no one to speak for her during the trial. A law passed in 1624 prosecuted women (in practice, intended to apply only to unmarried girls of lower class) whose babies had died, unless they could 'make proof by one witness at the least, that the child whose death was concealed was born dead'. This decree was exceptional in English law, since the accused was presumed guilty unless she could be proved innocent. It is thought that this law, together with Sir Thomas's wealth, reputation and power, ensured that Anne was found guilty by the jurors, who, of course, would all have been male and landed gentry.

The four doctors present at the dissection had their reputations made as a result of Anne's case, although Christopher Wren's involvement only became known a few years ago when his poem was discovered amongst thirty others written by the young Oxford undergraduates present. Among these is also a poem written by one Robert Matthews, Fellow of New College, and this was my starting point for the character of Robert, although I have no way of knowing if he had a stammer. It is said that Dr Willis had one, however, and ruminated on the cause of it.

Anne recovered very well from her ordeal, and her fame spread widely through the sale of pamphlets entitled 'Newes from the Dead', telling her story and giving speeches and prayers said to have been dictated by her. Generally, the people of the country felt that what had happened to her was God's miraculous way of saying she was innocent. The money collected at the apothecary's door from the hundreds who flocked to see her was used to pay for her pardon, and she became something of a celebrity, travelling up and down the country with her coffin and appearing in taverns and at fairs. She married soon after the event: the records merely say, 'Anne Green of Steeple Barton married John Taylor of Dun's Tew on the 29th May 1651', so I am guessing that she knew John beforehand, probably from when she worked for Sir Thomas in Dun's Tew. The couple were not married in Steeple Barton, however (Anne's home village), but in the larger church at Tadmarton, which lies a little further north. Perhaps the rector was unwilling to be a part of the fuss and excitement which would be bound to have accompanied such an event? However, Anne went on to have three children, and died in 1665.

What saved her from death? The instrument of hanging in those days was merely a noose from a tree or scaffold, without a trapdoor beneath, so the victim would have suffocated to death rather than have their neck broken, and the knot which should have pressed into Anne's throat may have been incorrectly placed. Perhaps most significant is the fact that on that day, 14 December 1650, it was fiercely cold, and it has been suggested that her suspended animation was due to something similar to cryogenic preservation, where the brain is frozen and thus prevented from being starved of oxygen.

BIBLIOGRAPHY

Burdet, W., *A Wonder of Wonders, being a faithful narrative and true relation of one Anne Green* (Oxford, 13 January 1651)

Fuller, Thomas, *History of the Worthies of England*: 'Sir Thomas Reade, Knight' (London, 1811)

Hewes, Gordon W., *Human Anatomy at Oxford in 1650: the role of future members of the Royal Society* (Paper given at the Conference on the History and Philosophy of Science, 28 April 1980)

Hughes, J. Trevor, *Miraculous Deliverance of Anne Green: an Oxford case of resuscitation in the 17th Century* (*British Medical Journal*, 285, 1982)

Oxford Dictionary of National Biography (Oxford University Press, 2004) for details of Drs Petty, Willis, Bathurst, Christopher Wren and Anne Green.

Pears, Ian, *An Instance of the Fingerpost* (Vintage, 1998)

Petty, William, ed. 6th Marquis of Lansdowne, *The Petty Papers*: William Petty's own notes on the case (London, 1924)

Plot, Robert, *The Natural History of Oxfordshire* (Oxford, 1677)

Robinson, Tho., *Newes from the Dead, or a True and Exact Narration of the miraculous deliverance of Anne Green*, printed by Leonard Lichfield (1651)

Walsham, Alexandra, *Providence in Early Modern England* (Clarendon Press, 1999)

Wood, Anthony A., *The Life and times of Anthony A. Wood, Antiquary of Oxford 1632–1695*, by himself (Oxford Historical Society)

Wrighton, Keith, *English Society 1580–1680* (Routledge, 2004)

Zimmer, Carl, *Soul Made Flesh: Thomas Willis, the Discovery of the Brain and How it Changed the World* (Heinemann, 2004)

The National Archives on-line: Oxford Circuit Assizes from 1627.

SET IN STONE

by LINDA NEWBERY

When naïve and impressionable artist Samuel Godwin
accepts the position of tutor to the daughters of
wealthy Ernest Farrow, he does not suspect that he's
walking into a web of deception. He is drawn into the lives
of three young women: Charlotte Agnew, the
governess; demure Juliana, the elder daughter, and her
passionate and wilful younger sister, Marianne, who
intrigues Samuel to the point of obsession.

And it's not just the people who entrance Samuel.
The house, Fourwinds, holds mysteries of its own,
and soon Samuel and Charlotte start to uncover
horrifying and dangerous secrets . . .

978 0 099 45133 4

a swift pure cry

by SIOBHAN DOWD

Life has been hard for Shell since the death of her mam.
Her dad has given up work and turned his back
on reality, leaving Shell to care for her brother and sister.
When she can, she spends time with her best friend
Bridie and the charming, persuasive Declan, sharing
cigarettes and irreverent jokes.

Shell is drawn to the kindness of Father Rose, a young
priest, but soon finds herself in the centre of an
escalating scandal that rocks the small Irish community
to its foundations.

'Beautifully written and deeply moving' *GUARDIAN*

978 0 099 48816 3

THE
MEDICI
SEAL

by THERESA BRESLIN

Italy, 1502

Fleeing from a murderous brigand, Matteo is taken
into the household of Leonardo da Vinci. And so he is at
the Maestro's side as da Vinci carries out his
work – work which ranges from military assignments
for the cruel Cesare Borgia to the painting of
magnificent frescos, experiments with flight and
the dissection of cadavers.

But Matteo carries with him a secret – a secret that both the
Borgia and the Medici families would kill to obtain . . .

'A superb historical thriller . . . an enchanting
novel about genius, and a gift to an enquiring mind'

THE TIMES

978 0 552 55447 3

VICTORY

by Susan Cooper

Sam Robbins is a farm boy, kidnapped and
forced to serve aboard HMS *Victory*, Lord Nelson's
ship at the Battle of Trafalgar in 1805. At first
Sam is terrified and seasick, but in a rowdy, dangerous
warship, he transforms himself into a sailor
and survives a fearsome and bloody battle, the echoes of
which reach through the years to touch Molly Jennings.
She is a modern-day English girl forced to live with
her new step-family in America, and she too is fighting a
battle against loss and loneliness.

This extraordinary time-shifting adventure tells the
interwoven stories of Sam and Molly, linked by
a mystery. Two lives joined for ever by the touch of
Nelson, one of the greatest sailors of all time.

978 0 552 55415 2